The Captive Saga

The Captive Saga

Book Two

"Captive Fear"

Amazing Grace Williams

This is a work of fiction. Names, characters, places and incidents either are the product of the author's imagination or are used fictitiously, and any resemblance to any actual persons, living or dead, events, or locales is entirely coincidental.

This book was printed in the United States of America.

To order additional copies of this book, contact:
Xlibris Corporation
1-888-795-4274
www.Xlibris.com
Orders@Xlibris.com
112612

For Tonya Dawn Hilburn,
my sister, my friend

1 Peter 5:7
Casting all your care upon him; for he careth for you.

Table of Contents

Chapter 1

"Stunned Sorrow"

BREU MADE AUBREY leave the inside of the Whitton house by hurriedly and forcefully escorting her outside. Charles and Clara's home was swarmed by townspeople who quickly heard about the commotion, both inside and out. Women were crying, men were sighing and shaking their heads from side to side in pain for their friends.

"Go get the undertaker," Breu commanded one of the men who stood outside.

He held Aubrey tightly while she sobbed into his chest. She couldn't think, she couldn't breathe, she couldn't see through all of her tears. Her own brother Marty just committed suicide, because he desired to die for his crimes against her and others by his own hand, rather than face a judge.

Clara clung to her dead son's body. Aubrey and Breu could both hear her agonizing screams and gasps for air. Marty's blood was getting all over Clara's nice dress she saved to wear for the celebration. She didn't care, because she had not seen her son since he was fifteen, and after tonight, Clara would never be able to see him again.

Through Clara's tears, she gazed into Marty's face. He did not look like a young boy anymore, as he had the last time she saw him. Instead, Marty looked like a man, more long and broad than what she remembered. She noticed that he had even lost his boyish face and gained a man's. She gently stroked her son's head, though she knew he could not feel her gentle touch, smearing the tears and blood in his hair.

No one was going to deprive Clara of this last chance to hold her son, although it was torturing not only her, but the onlookers as well. Men could see Marty's blood staining Clara's dress more and more, but none of them would budge so they might help her up. All they could do was stand there and watch, trying to hold back tears of their own.

Charles was in a stand still as well. He did not cry at seeing his dead son lying there on his floor, but could only seem to stare at his Marty's body, looking at him from head to toe as if to be examining him. Charles was not going to make his wife leave Marty just yet either, because if he did, she would most likely hate him for it. Charles was stunned, almost to the point of not being able to move.

He felt as though he needed to do something, but he couldn't. A few men who were inside the Whitton cabin had enough of the gruesome sight, so they walked slowly back outside, making room for others who wanted to intrude to see what the torturous scene looked like.

Once inside, a few wished that they hadn't come in. Marty's head still seeped blood, but what had been out in the open for a while now, including on Clara's dress, was drying fast. Back outside, the once peaceful and quiet ambience of the Whitton property was that of low talking and whispers. Usually one could sense an unexplainable peace and joy when coming to the Whitton cabin, but on this evening, everyone felt sorrow and heartache.

Breu still held Aubrey tightly, and at times her sobs would cease, but then she would replay the previous events, making her sobbing begin again. Breu honestly was like Charles and did not know what to do, so he stood there and kept holding Aubrey, patiently waiting for the undertaker to arrive.

The sun was almost out of sight now, barely putting forth any sort of light. There were some men lighting lanterns outside that had been pulled from their wagons. Stunned sorrow was in the air, and everyone could feel it. What seemed like several hours was really only about forty-five minutes.

Finally, after this excruciating and seemingly long wait, the undertaker arrived driving a wagon. He pulled up his wagon near the door of the Whitton cabin, and then Charles made Clara leave Marty's side with all the gentleness he could find. Clara seemed to be a little calmer when she stood to her feet, but as men began lifting Marty's lifeless body, she lost all control.

"Marty, Marty, my baby!" she cried as she staggered out of the cabin after the undertaker.

Clara could not contain her emotions, but had to follow her firstborn. Seeing this made every eye that looked upon her tear up, including Breu. Charles followed Clara, but could do absolutely nothing to calm her emotions. He finally realized that the only thing he could do is be by her side.

After the men delicately placed Marty onto the undertaker's wagon, Clara climbed onto the back of it as well, making everyone who watched gasp. Charles couldn't believe what he was seeing.

"Clara, get down now," he said trying to be sensitive. "We'll follow in our wagon."

Charles reached for Clara to help her down, but she jerked her body away from him and shouted, "No! After tomorrow I'm never going to see my baby again! I'm going to ride with him and spend time with him." Tears freely fell from her eyes like raindrops falling from the sky. Charles hesitated before he said anything more, but felt that he had to at least try one more time to get his wife away from his son's dead body.

"Marty isn't there Clara, you have to let him go."

"Well if it's so easy for you, then let me go!" she shouted, this time in anger.

Charles sighed, looked at Clara with tortured eyes, and then turned in defeat to go get his wagon so he could follow the undertaker into town. Upon seeing this and hearing the pain in her mother's voice, Aubrey cried even more. She had to get away, so she tried to break free from her fiancé's grip and run to an isolated place in the darkness. Breu grabbed her arm, and led Aubrey back into the cabin across the blood-stained floor. He took her into her bedroom and told her to stay there until he made everybody leave.

Aubrey could do nothing but fall onto her bed, bury her face into the covers, and gasp for air through her sobs. The undertaker started to leave with Clara holding onto Marty in the back, and Charles following solemnly behind. Breu started clearing out the crowd, telling them that there was nothing left to see.

Slowly everyone reluctantly got back into their wagons, or back on their horses, and began leaving as well. Some did not know whether to go back to the celebration, or just go home. Finally, none were left save Aubrey and Breu. When he watched the last person leave he came inside the cabin, and found Aubrey trying to wipe up Marty's blood from the wood floor.

Her beautiful dress was dirty and wet from the snow, with blood stains on it now from the chore she was doing. While Breu made people leave, she had gathered the strength to find a towel and begin wiping up the blood, though the stain was fiercely evident. She sniffled as she said, "I have to do this for mama. She won't be able to do this."

Breu could see that she was trying to help Clara, but he also saw that Aubrey had to do this to get busy, so maybe she would not go crazy. He wished with all of his might that he could erase the fatal and devastating events of this night, but Breu knew that this was impossible, so instead he earnestly prayed. Breu could have made Aubrey stop what she was doing and leave with him, but he chose instead to get down on his knees beside her and help Aubrey clean up the blood. He knew that this would most definitely be the better thing to do.

Breu tried not to say much, for the fear of saying the wrong thing. They finished cleaning all they could clean, then Breu took Aubrey into his arms and said a prayer. The Lord would have to take over from here, because this situation was more than anyone humanly knew how to deal with. Breu now realized that he was going to have to be a strong anchor for Aubrey, especially if he planned to marry her.

After praying, Breu helped Aubrey up and led her to the wagon when he closed the door. They took off, heading back to Moline, leaving the Whitton cabin in an eerie silence. The townspeople who returned to the church for the celebration did not celebrate, but instead all joined hands in prayer for the Whittons. Afterward, everyone stood around and visited, with the absent yet faithful family possessing their conversations.

Most of the women discussed what dish each would prepare and bring to Clara and Charles, since the funeral would obviously be the next day. No one wanted to bring the same thing, so each lady of the church decided on a specific food to supply.

"I can't believe this happened," Aubrey kept saying over and over again as she rode beside Breu, not even realizing that she was repeating herself.

Breu wrapped his arm around her and squeezed her tightly. In the back of the undertaker's wagon, Clara held onto Marty, caressing his hair, and covering him back up when the blanket slipped down, the way she used to do when he was a little child.

The undertaker tried his best to focus on the road despite the constant cries, gasps, and wails that he heard from Clara. Charles rode on behind Clara and the undertaker, being completely stunned and shocked by everything that happened, but he tried his hardest to put his emotions aside, and figure out a way to get Clara away from Marty, as he feared this would be very difficult.

When Breu, the undertaker, and all of the Whittons arrived in Moline very little was spoken, however a large plain wooden coffin was decided upon for the funeral, as well as a time. Clara requested that Marty's service at the grave begin at two o' clock, so she could have one more morning with her son. All she wanted was more time with her son, as if what little time she would be able to have with him could make up for all of the time she had lost.

"And where will we bury Mr. Whitton?" the undertaker professionally asked.

Clara and Charles looked at each other and said nothing for a moment. At different points in time during their happy marriage, Charles and Clara had discussed a burying ground for their bodies, but never once did they think that a child would be buried there before them.

The Whittons owned one-hundred acres of lush beautiful green land, with hills and fields galore, so breath-taking at times during any season. There was a meadow amidst all of their property, that bloomed vibrant vivacious hues during the spring and summer, and this was the place where Charles and Clara had always pictured their graves. Both knew what the other was thinking, and then Charles softly answered.

"He will be buried in the meadow that lies in the middle of our property."

Clara began to pour a waterfall of tears at her husband's soft yet firm reply.

The undertaker nodded his head in compliance and said, "I will send my men to begin digging first thing in the morning so that his grave will be ready by two."

Charles and Breu carried Marty's lifeless body into the morgue, and when Aubrey looked up about ten minutes later, she saw them carrying out a large wooden coffin. She stayed close to her mother and tried not to lose control of her feelings, though Clara had already lost hers at the sight of the wooden box.

The men loaded the coffin onto Charles and Clara's wagon, and without any thought, hesitation, or opposition, Clara once again climbed into the back of the wagon, setting down beside Marty. Charles just let her be. He realized that if he tried to make a mother leave her child's dead body, then he would most likely have a very angry tigress on his hands.

Charles' only thought now was of getting his family home. Breu wanted to be close to Aubrey, and his dear friends and future in-laws, to make sure they were alright, so he led Aubrey back to his wagon and helped her up onto the seat.

"I'll take you back home," he said.

The ride home was cold, confusing, and nearly hours long it seemed. Charles and Clara did not say a word, while Breu and Aubrey barely spoke themselves.

Soon everyone arrived safely back at the cabin. It looked just the way it had when they left it, though the darkness prohibited everyone's normal vision. Aubrey and Clara made a space for Marty's coffin to rest for the night in the main room of the cabin, while Breu and Charles brought him inside.

Once the coffin was settled in, everyone sat down and sighed as if they were in a daze. Clara could not take her eyes off of the coffin, while Aubrey looked back and forth from it, to her parents, and then at Breu.

Breu was honestly the only one in the room at this moment who had his wits about him, but they were being focused on the family whose cabin he resided at presently.

"What a way to start a new year," Breu thought to himself.

Beside his own people, Breu had never before seen a family suffer as much as the Whittons had up until now, but even some of his own family was not allowed to live long enough to possibly go through this kind of pain.

He sat in the home of the Whittons for a while, to make sure they would be alright. Hardly a word was spoken the entire time, but Breu had to break the eerie silence.

"If there is anything you need, anything I can do just let me know."

"Thank you Breu," Charles replied. "Thanks for staying with us." Breu motioned for Aubrey to follow him outside.

"I have to get back to Moline Aubrey, but I want you to promise me that if anything happens, you'll come get me."

"I promise," she said looking into his eyes.

"I love you Aubrey, and I'll be back to check on you all."

The truth was that Breu was extremely reluctant to go, but being the sheriff, he had to get back to his post.

"I love you too."

Breu leaned into her ear and whispered, "For what it's worth, happy new year."

He gave Aubrey a tight squeeze followed with a short but meaningful kiss, then turned to go.

Aubrey stood there watching him leave, and then quietly whispered, "Happy new year."

Aubrey glanced down at the ground, and through the heavy darkness, she could see a dark trail of spots in the snow that led out of the house. With a little bit of light shining down from the moon, Aubrey could tell that it was blood. Breu prayed the whole way back to the sheriff's office. Aubrey sluggishly went back into the house to see her parents still sitting down in silence. Normally Aubrey would have been extremely sad with

Breu's departure, but concern for her mama and papa easily prevailed this night. As she stood there watching her parents Charles stood and said,

"Well, there is nothing more we can do tonight. We all need to go to bed and get some rest."

Though she feared sleep and rest would not easily come, Aubrey was all for lying down in her comfortable bed. Aubrey walked over to the door that led to her room, but Clara stayed right where she was, never budging. Charles and Aubrey stopped before they entered their rooms, turning to see if Clara would follow.

"You need to get some sleep. Are you coming?" Charles asked his wife.

"Do you really think I'll get any sleep tonight Charles? I'm content where I am, and this is where I am going to stay."

Aubrey raised her eyebrows at her mother's defiance, though Aubrey figured that she would most likely have replied the same way. Charles exhaled heavily, wanting desperately to argue, and even contemplating about it, but he knew he would not win.

Again he sighed heavily, shaking his head in defeat as he entered into his room. Aubrey did not know what to say, if she should say anything, so giving her mother one last glance she also turned and entered her room. Now it was just Clara and her dead son alone. When she heard Aubrey and Charles climb into their beds Clara stood to her feet, walked over and added more wood to the dying fire, then went to the wooden box and lifted the lid.

As soon as Marty's pale face came into view, Clara covered her mouth with her trembling hand, feeling tears flow down her cheeks. She had to sit back in the chair again for fear of collapsing. Clara could not, and would not take her eyes off of her son. She wanted so badly to brand his face in her mind so she would not forget what he looked like as a man, because tomorrow would be the last time she would ever get to see him again while on this earth, and this being the only time she had ever seen him as a man.

If Clara imprinted his face in her memory, then never again would she have to wonder what he looked like. Never again would Clara wonder if he looked like his papa did when he was young, or if he still carried most of her features like he did as a child. All Clara could think of right now, was "Why?"

Why did Marty kill himself? Why did he do this to his own family and kidnap his own sister? Why did he choose to live his life this way, when he was raised better? Why did Marty leave home to begin with? These questions Clara could not understand, but then Proverbs chapter three and verse five came to her troubled mind.

"Trust in the Lord with all thine heart; and lean not unto thine own understanding."

This would be a long difficult road Clara would have to travel, just as Aubrey would have to do with putting her faith and trust in God with her protection and peace of mind. Clara left the coffin's lid open, and wetted a rag to clean Marty's face.

There was nothing she could do for the rest of him, but she could at least make his face presentable, though she would be the only one to see it. Clara would cry a while, sit down and stare at Marty lying in his coffin, then cry for a while more. This went on all night long. Never before in her life had she felt so isolated and desolate than right now. She knew God was with her, but right now she felt alone.

At times Clara even fought sleep, but fight it she did, because she did not want to miss one second with her son. While she was awake Clara was in a melancholy fog. She did not appreciate the warmth that the fire gave like she usually would have, nor did she see anything else that existed in the room, save for Marty, and the blood stain on the floor. She could not take her eyes off of it at times, just staring at it as if the stain were a snake, being unable to go near it.

At one point in time early in the morning, Clara heard a scratching on the door followed by some very faint sounds. Deciding she could use the little walk over to the window to stretch her legs, Clara got up. There was a curious, poor looking feline sitting at the door. Clara knew what it wanted, but its request would not be granted tonight, especially with her son's body.

This night was absolutely agonizing. Clara honestly did not know what to do with herself. She spent the entire night alternating from crying, to sitting, to pacing the floor, while fighting sleep and exhaustion with it all. Aubrey tossed and turned, but eventually a light, rough sleep found her. Despite the light sleep she was able to manage, Aubrey dreamed of Marty and everything that previously happened. Off and on she would awaken to be drenched in sweat, even though her room was cool. Charles lay in his bed, and had let his tears freely flow until they soaked his pillowcase. Now that his entire family was safe at home, he could let his emotions loose, but he had to get it out before morning, because then he would need to be strong for Clara and Aubrey.

Charles finally fell asleep after lying in his bed for a few hours. Many times before then however, Charles wanted to go check on his wife, but he knew that she needed some space right now.

Before Clara knew, she had fallen asleep along with the rest of the household, and morning had come. Charles woke Clara by making coffee, obviously not meaning to, but both believed that the previous night was the longest one they had ever known. Clara noticed that the lid to Marty's coffin was closed. She did not do it, so she assumed that Charles must have done it. Not wanting to start an argument, and frankly not having any energy to even speak, Clara got up, walked over to Marty, and opened the lid once more.

Everyone felt like a snail, and moved almost as slow as one throughout the day. Aubrey and Charles did all of the morning chores, trying their best to help Clara as much as they could because they knew she had not gotten much rest. At one point in the morning, the gravediggers came, so Charles had to stop what he was doing to take them to the meadow and show them where Marty's grave was to be. At dinner time, none felt like eating, but Aubrey fixed a small meal of leftover meat and beans so their stomachs would not be entirely empty.

Soon, the undertaker arrived with his wagon, and it was nearly two o' clock. Breu followed him inside the cabin after arriving next, and helped Charles move the coffin back onto the wagon. When the coffin was moved, Clara and Aubrey went into their bedrooms to change their dresses and freshen up.

Aubrey and Clara came out after about ten minutes, ready to go to the funeral. Clara was not emotionally prepared for this, but she knew that there was nothing she could do to stop it. She climbed onto the wagon with Charles, while Aubrey got onto Breu's.

Charles led the way, and they began making their way to the snow-covered meadow. Clara was numb to her surroundings. On any other day she would have enjoyed this ride, the fresh air, the gorgeous scenery, but today she only stared straight ahead of herself, not paying heed to what was happening around her.

All Aubrey was concerned about was her mother. She had nearly gotten over the realization of almost being in a shootout the night before, but she had never seen her own mother in such a state of sorrow. It scared Aubrey. Charles seemed to be handling the situation well, so Clara is who obsessed Aubrey's concerns and cares. Breu was unsure of how to approach Aubrey covertly, to find out how she was truly handling this.

After riding for a short while he finally asked, "How are your mama and papa doing so far?"

If Breu could just get Aubrey talking, then he could see how she was.

"Mama stayed up all night with the body. Papa is just trying not to do anything to upset her. I'm pretty sure I heard him sniffling last night."

"Did you get any sleep?"

"A little."

Word had quickly spread around town as to where Marty would be buried, and at what time, so when Breu and the Whittons arrived in the meadow, there was already a very large crowd waiting on them. Charles, Clara, and Aubrey were surprised by this large group of people, so much so that Aubrey's mouth dropped open.

The people moved aside to let the wagons through, and then shortly Charles and Breu got out the coffin, and placed it in the freshly dug hole in the ground. The Whittons, Breu, and the preacher assumed there positions around the grave, then the service began.

Aubrey hardly heard a word the preacher said. She was lost in thought of the previous events of her kidnapping, and now the burial of her brother.

"That's just it," she thought. "He is my brother, and I don't even know him. I don't know his successes, his failures, or his favorite color."

But worst of all, Aubrey did not know where Marty was beginning to spend his eternity. Not hearing anything or anyone beside her own thought, Aubrey just stood there next to Clara, staring down at the wooden box, trying to remember something from her childhood that involved Marty. She began to get a headache from thinking so hard, but every memory she went through, Marty was not there.

Though this man was a fugitive, he was still her brother, and it began to make Aubrey angry that she did not know him at all. At this point, all Aubrey knew was Marty's name, and what he looked like. For Aubrey, the only legacy Marty left behind was that of a thief, kidnapper, and even murderer. She knew there had to be more to Marty's life than just rebellion and lawlessness, but Aubrey feared that it would never be revealed to her.

It was very cold outside with gray clouds covering the entire sky, matching the mood of the day. Yesterday's events had not yet completely sunk in with the Whittons, because each was in their own little world of confusion, regret, and sorrow. Each were dwelling upon different things, each feeling the same emotions, just in separate ways.

The service finally ended, and everyone began stirring and moving around, except for Charles, Clara, and Aubrey. Charles came back to his senses, and then led Clara back to the wagon. As Aubrey began following behind, a hand gently grabbed her arm turning her around. The hand belonged to Dr. Starks.

"Aubrey, I am terribly sorry for your loss. I just wanted to let you know that I understand if you aren't able to begin working yet. You will always have a job when you are ready."

Aubrey was very appreciative to Dr. Starks for his compassion.

"Thank you," was all she could manage to say.

She turned once more in the direction of the wagon, with Breu walking by her side. Clara wanted to stay longer in the meadow, but not with so many people there. She wanted to be alone by her son's fresh grave, so Clara decided that she would return later in the day.

When the Whittons returned home, they were surprised to see people coming to their cabin who had just been with them at the funeral. They weren't particularly in the mood for company, but Charles and Clara were not the type to be rude. As people were getting off of their wagons, they were also retrieving different food items the women had recently prepared. Cobblers, dressings, casseroles, and pies were the main dishes brought into the Whitton cabin.

Even Laura Woods and Rose Bennett brought food for Charles and Clara, but neither lady acknowledged that the other was there, or even existed for that matter. Since they spent sometime in jail for their disruptive behavior, Laura and Rose did not go out of their way to do something that would upset the other, but they still did not speak, or show any kind of civility to the other. Howbeit they were both faithful in church and completely convinced that the other was in the wrong.

Rose Bennett was reluctant to even come to the funeral, which had it not been one, her presence there wouldn't have existed. Being unknown by the Whittons, Rose had a distain for them, but they weren't the only ones Rose felt this way about. She had no decent reasoning behind her distain, but Rose didn't need any. Nevertheless, she came and brought a dish, but mainly so Laura Woods would not beat her out of performing a kindness.

Charles and Clara thanked everyone who stopped by and handed them food, and accepted the dishes as gracefully as possible for such tragic circumstances. As hard as Clara tried, she could not force a smile, and told herself that they would just have to understand. She wasn't in the mood, and had not the capability to act like she was in good spirits.

When Aubrey and Breu arrived, she did not know what to do with herself. Aubrey was feeling so many different emotions at the same time such as grief, disappointment, concern, confusion, and more. Not knowing what else to do, she began helping her mother put away and sort all of the food.

Aubrey felt awkward right now in her own home. One reason was because she had never seen Clara and Charles in this state before, and the other reason was because she felt somewhat responsible for Marty's death. Though Aubrey did not realize it at the moment, she felt like she was responsible for the pain and heartache her mama and papa were feeling.

Aubrey did not understand why God had allowed all of this to happen. This was the sort of thing she heard happening to other people, but this happened to her family. Nothing like this had ever taken place before in Moline, at least while Aubrey was alive.

Why her? Why her family? These questions were ever present in Aubrey's mind. She knew, and had always been taught that God is in control, with there being a reason for everything. Aubrey could very plainly see that from here on out, if she or her family was going to overcome this trial, then their faith and trust would have to be placed in the Lord's hands continuously.

She had always believed her faith to be strong and unyielding, until now. Aubrey could not understand why before these unexpected events, she had been a strong Christian, but now her spiritual world seemed to be falling apart.

What scared Aubrey though was the silence of her mother. She did not know what Clara was thinking, feeling, or if she blamed Aubrey for her son's death. Not a word was spoken between the two as they put away all of the food, and Aubrey was getting desperate to hear something, anything from Clara.

Several times Aubrey almost said something to her mother, but just as the words were at the tip of her tongue she stopped, surrendering to the silence again. She felt her safety net being yanked out from under her. Aubrey understood that her mother was hurting, but fear was now controlling Aubrey. Fear of never being able to stand it staying alone by herself, fear of her faith in God never being strong again, and fear of being blamed for the sudden death of her long lost brother, by two of the very few people she could confide in, her own parents.

Chapter 2

"Stains and the Hotel"

FINALLY THE LAST wagon left and things began to calm down, however Clara could not seem to stop looking at the blood stains on her floor. She tried desperately to get her eyes and mind on something else, but Clara was quickly becoming restless inside the cabin because there was really another place she wanted to be, in the meadow.

Clara began looking around the cabin for a rug to place over the stained part of the floor, and soon she found one.

"Maybe this will ease my heart," she thought to herself as she covered the troublesome sight.

She thought that she would wait another hour or so before she returned to the meadow, hoping to find that the rug being there on her floor would help her forget what lied underneath.

She never spoke a word during all of this, but Charles and Aubrey watched her, understanding without her having to say anything why she did what she did. The rug however was not helping, because during that whole next hour, Clara found herself still glancing constantly at the rug, picturing in her mind the blood stained floor.

Having had enough, Clara could not take being inside her cabin for another minute. She slowly got up from the rocking chair she sat in, and walked over to where her coat hung.

"I'm going back to the meadow," she solemnly announced. Charles stood to his feet, but Clara finished, "I'd rather be alone."

"Well let me at least get the wagon ready for you."

Clara desired to walk to the meadow, but she knew that with the cold weather and long distance, this would not be the wisest thing to do, so she let Charles go. Aubrey wanted badly to go with her mother, to stay by her side and be the support Clara needed, but Aubrey could not even speak to her. She opened her mouth, but again was only submissive to silence.

Charles drove the wagon to the front door of the cabin, and when he faced Clara he said, "Don't stay gone too long."

She only stared back at him, then climbed onto the wagon and left. When Clara was out of sight, Aubrey walked over to the worn old bluish gray rug and looked down at it while she thought. Charles added more wood to the fire.

Aubrey walked over to the kitchen. She grabbed a large bowl and filled it with warm soapy water. Charles now became curious as to what she was up to. After going back to the rug, she removed it, knelt down, and started scrubbing away at the blood stain.

She thought that if she could make the blood stains disappear, then maybe some of her mother's pain and heartache would vanish along with it. The stain however was not going anywhere, so Aubrey scrubbed even harder, in vain.

"It's no use," Charles said.

Aubrey stopped scrubbing and sighed.

"I thought I'd try. You know that's what is bothering her right?"

"I know, but that stain isn't going anywhere."

Charles wasn't being coldhearted, but rather was stating fact and reality. Charles never was the type to go around pretending. Aubrey sat back in defeat and sighed. Now to accompany the still dark blood stain was a large spot of water.

All she could do now was dispose of the soapy water, keep the rug off of the wet spot on the floor so it could dry, and pray that God would give each of them His peace that passeth all understanding.

The entire ride to the meadow Clara wanted desperately to talk to God, but when she tried, she could not stop sobbing. Her heart ached for God's touch, but she could not get out a single word. Clara knew however that God understood her heart, and that she did not have to say anything for God to know what she was feeling.

After all, she was reminded, God suffered this same pain before Clara did, so He knew exactly what she was feeling. Clara had never realized until now, just what God sacrificed when He sent Jesus. A part of her wanted to be angry with God for what He was allowing her to go through, but she couldn't. How could she be angry with Him, when He willingly gave His son as a sacrifice?

No, this was a choice, and Clara chose to rely on God rather than be angry and resentful. She would pray every minute of everyday if she had to, but Clara made up her mind as she sat beside Marty's grave, that she would get through this. Clara knew she had to be strong for her family.

All of her life Clara had known different folks who had lost children, and she always hoped that she would never have to suffer through the pain she saw them tormented with.

"I don't know if I can do this," she thought as she placed her hand onto the grave.

But then all of a sudden Clara began to feel a peace come over her that she understood to be from her Heavenly Father. She stayed by Marty's fresh grave until the sun was bidding its goodnight to Clara's side of the earth. Her hands were dirty from rubbing and patting the earth that now covered her son's body, but she had to get back to the cabin before the sun completely disappeared on her.

The ride from the grave was no easier than the ride to it, but Clara had faith in God that over time, everything would be alright, and He was already blessing her with the strength she needed to get through this day. If she was gone for too much longer then Charles was going to go looking for her, but a little while after deciding this he could hear someone in a wagon coming near the cabin.

Aubrey sighed in relief when she saw her mother enter the cabin a little while later. Clara did not remove her coat upon entering the door, but instead went straight into her bedroom. She did not believe that she could stay any longer in her own home, so Clara got out her small suitcase, and quietly began packing it with her clothes. She had made a decision while riding back to the cabin, and no one was going to stop her from seeing it through. Charles joined her in the bedroom after curiosity got the best of him when Clara didn't come back out.

"What are you doing?" he asked as he watched his wife pack.

"I don't think I can stay here," she replied.

"What? What do you mean?"

Charles was now alarmed.

"I just can't stay here with that blood stain on the floor. I thought I could, but it will drive me crazy. I can't stop looking at it, even with the rug there. That's why I put it there, because I thought it would help, but its not."

"Where do you plan on going?"

Clara shook her head as she thought.

"I guess I'll stay at the hotel in Moline."

"C'mon Clara, don't do that. Stay here."

"I need some time away Charles. Please understand."

"The stain will always be there, so what do you plan on doing next? You can't live in the hotel."

"I don't know Charles!" Clara said loudly.

Taking in a deep breath, she continued.

"I just need to get away from here for a few days, and I'll figure things out while I'm gone."

"Well you're not going alone," Charles informed.

"I didn't want to. I was hoping you would come with me. I need you Charles."

He sighed, realizing that there was no way to change Clara's mind.

"Alright," he finally said.

Walking back into the living room of the cabin, Charles was going to tell Aubrey what he and Clara were about to do, because he knew that Aubrey was not going to stay home alone, and he honestly didn't want her to.

"Your mother doesn't want to stay here, so we are going to check into the hotel. Pack your things and come with us."

Aubrey was taken by complete surprise.

"When are we coming back?"

"I don't know yet, but hurry up and get your things."

Aubrey wanted to ask more questions but was afraid to. Quickly her mind started whirling, trying to sort out what was going on and what she could do to ease her parents' burdens. Suddenly something hit her.

"I can't stay in the same room with you both, and there is no sense in getting another room, so maybe Esther will let me stay with her."

"That's fine."

Aubrey went to hurriedly pack her suitcase, hoping that Esther would have enough room. Esther Jones had been among the many who attended Marty's funeral, and gloomy sorrow lingered with her due to the pain her best friend was now plagued with. She sat by the fireplace that burned within her room, sipping on a cup of hot coffee when she heard someone gently tapping on her door.

"Who on earth could that be?" she asked herself. As she got up and walked over to the door Esther shouted, "Store's closed till the morning." When she opened the door she saw Aubrey standing there with a suitcase in her hand.

"Child what are you doing?" Esther asked in confusion. "Get in here out of this cold," she continued as she brought Aubrey inside her room.

Esther saw no one with her dear friend's daughter, but she knew that something wasn't right.

"Now what's got you out here this time of night all by yourself?"

Aubrey's teeth chattered as she stood by the fire to get warm, but she tried to calm them down as she replied, "Mama and papa are staying in the hotel tonight. Mama can't stand to be in the house with Marty's blood stained on the floor."

"Goodness gracious child!"

"I was hoping, if you can spare the room, could I stay here? I didn't see a point in wasting money on another hotel room when I could stay with you."

"Well of course Aubrey. I'd much rather have you here than the hotel. But tell me, do you think this is temporary, or can your mama make it the rest of her days in the cabin her son was killed in?"

Aubrey sighed, thinking deeply and hard for the answer to Esther's question, but all she could say was, "I don't know."

In Aubrey's heart she hoped for the best, but feared the worst. What if her mama couldn't stand to go back to the cabin? Where would they live? What would they do? Her papa's goldmine, along with all of their memories was there, as well as her brother's body.

The future was now so uncertain. Aubrey thought she had control of her life and what was going to happen in it, like working for the doctor, marrying Breu, and spending the rest of her life in Moline, but it seemed as though a tornado of destruction had ripped right through Aubrey's life, only leaving bits and pieces of what she knew, and who she thought she was.

Esther could easily see that Aubrey was tired, dazed, and scared. She realized that this may take along while, but God would work everything out for His honor and glory. In the meantime, she knew who was going to be at the top of her prayer list until then, the Whittons.

Aubrey did not know what she would do tomorrow. She longed to be with her mother, to know how she was doing, what she thinking, and if she placed any of the guilt on Aubrey for what was done. Being apart from Clara was torturous right now, but Aubrey wanted to give her mama some space because she most probably needed it.

Esther let Aubrey share her bed, and soon Aubrey was asleep while Esther still sat by the fire. Clara and Charles quickly fell asleep as well after checking into their hotel room and getting everything situated inside. Well needed prayers reached Heaven that night for the Whittons, with

Esther and Breu keeping a constant prayer for them on their minds. Just like the regular cycle of the earth however, nighttime went on, eventually yielding to the sun's morning rays without any concern for the sorrowed and exhausted.

AMAZING GRACE WILLIAMS

Chapter 3

"Blame and Gossip"

AUBREY AWOKE EARLY to find Esther gone. Though her eyes remained heavy, Aubrey got up and refreshed herself by washing her face with icy cold water, to her body's horror, and fixed her hair the best she could with what she had. Aubrey was familiar with the layout of the building she was in because Aubrey had grown up around it, so without a second thought Aubrey pushed open the door that joined the store and Esther's room. This led to where Esther stood a lot of the day, behind the counter, and just as Aubrey suspected Esther was there helping customers.

"Good morning child," Esther said loudly drawing the customer's attention to Aubrey.

Some of them had been at the funeral, while the others must have been strangers passing through because Aubrey didn't recall ever seeing them before.

The store was busy this morning, and Aubrey had no idea what to do with herself, so she came to Esther's side and asked, "Is there anything I can do?"

"Why sure honey, but first I want you to go over to the hotel and see if your mama and papa need anything."

"Alright then, I'll be back."

Aubrey couldn't believe she didn't think to go check on her parents this morning. "That should have been the first thing on my mind!" she thought. "I must still be asleep." A part of her feared to see the condition of her mama and papa, but Aubrey knew she had to be strong. After a short walk in the snowy cold, Aubrey entered the hotel and asked the clerk which room the Whittons were occupying.

"Room seven," the clerk said.

"Hmm," Aubrey thought, "God's perfect number."

When she reached the door that was marked seven, Aubrey gently tapped with her cold knuckles. There was no answer. She tapped again, a little harder this time, and quietly waited. They wouldn't have left without telling her, and the clerk would have said that they checked out if they had, but where could they be?

"What could they have to do in town?" Aubrey thought as she kept waiting.

Finally, Aubrey straightened up her posture as she heard someone approaching from the other side of the door. As it slowly opened Charles came into view, and he told Aubrey to come in.

Upon entering, Aubrey saw that the bed was neatly made, the red draperies were pulled back to let in the sunlight, and Charles folding up the newspaper he had been reading.

"Where's mama?" she thought it safe to ask.

"She went downstairs to the restaurant to have some breakfast."

"You're not going to eat?"

"Not right now," Charles said shrugging his shoulders. "I'll eat at dinner."

"How's mama doing?"

"Alright I guess. We may be here another night or two." Aubrey's eyes widened.

"What are you going to do papa?"

"I don't know yet, but we can't live here that's for sure."

Aubrey didn't want to agitate her papa by asking more questions, because she could see that he was still extremely tired.

"What are your plans?" he asked.

"I guess I'll help Esther in the store today. She said I could and right now it's pretty busy in there." Charles nodded his head.

"She wanted to know if you needed anything."

Charles thought before he spoke but said, "I can't think of anything at the moment, but we'll probably be stopping by, even if it's for just a visit."

"Alright, well let me know if you need anything, or if your plans change."

"We will. Same to you."

"Love you papa."

"Love you too."

Aubrey turned to go, not wanting to, but realizing that she had to be a big girl and find the strength she needed to get through, without having to rely on her parents dwindling strength.

Things were so different now. Before, if something like this happened, she was right with her folks, leaning on them to survive, but now that she was grown Aubrey had to learn to lean not on her parents, but on God, and that scared her. Aubrey's life, and everything she knew was slowly changing uncontrollably, leaving Aubrey filling like she was in a scattered wind being blown here and there.

As she left the hotel, Aubrey thought about going to see her mother, but fear struck her with the possibility of Clara being angry with her. She decided that she would give Clara more time to herself, just in case, though Aubrey longed to be held by her mother like when she was just a child.

While walking across the street, one more person crossed Aubrey's mind who she hadn't even thought about till now, Breu. He probably still figured that the Whittons were home. Before going back to Esther's store, Aubrey decided to make a short visit to the jail, to let Breu know what was going on, just in case he tried to make an unnecessary trip out to the cabin.

To Aubrey's relief, Breu was in his office doing paperwork. He did not expect to see Aubrey step inside his door.

"Aubrey?" he said in alarm at seeing her presence. "Is everything alright?"

"Yes," she replied hastily, trying to ease Breu's worried mind. "I just wanted to let you know that we are staying here in town, just in case you intended on coming out to the cabin. Mama and papa are at the hotel, but I am with Esther. Papa said that they may stay in town for a few more days, which means that I will as well."

Breu listened carefully to the words his fiancé was saying, but being unable to explain it, Breu felt and saw a sudden change in Aubrey. He realized that she had recently been through very traumatic events, but something about Aubrey was now different, and it sort of scared him. When Aubrey finished speaking she turned to leave, but Breu stopped her.

"Aubrey wait," he beckoned catching her arm and pulling her close to him. "Are you alright?"

He looked down on her face, deeply into her eyes. Aubrey couldn't bring herself to pour out her feelings to Breu. Without even knowing it, Aubrey was completely blaming herself for everything that happened, while being afraid the whole time that her mother was as well. She felt her eyes sting with tears, but she would not let them fall.

"I'm fine," she said trying to smile, but her efforts could not keep Breu from seeing that there was something terribly wrong. "I've got to go. I promised Esther I would help her in the store today."

Before Breu could even attempt a kiss, Aubrey pulled away from him and was gone. All he could do was stand there stunned. This wasn't right. Aubrey wasn't acting like her normal self. Breu could easily see that things were changing, but he couldn't tell if they were changing for the good, or bad.

Aubrey hurriedly walked down the street. She pulled away from Breu for a reason, but she couldn't seem to find it. All she knew was that she had to get busy in Esther's store, to keep her mind off of what was happening. To Aubrey, everything seemed to be spinning out of control, like tumbleweed being blown by the hot desert wind. Maybe soon, she hoped, her life would get back to the way it was.

Everyone in town must have gotten back to their daily routines, without another thought otherwise, but Aubrey was held captive by her sorrow, fear, and guilt. When would she stop feeling this way? When would she be assured of her mother's well-being, and free of her mother's blame?

So many times Aubrey felt tears swell up in her eyes, but Aubrey would not allow herself to cry. She told herself that she had to be strong. Having not known her brother, save only a few things, the thought of being the cause of his death was almost more than Aubrey could bear. She had seen the way Clara acted with Marty's dead body, and the more she pondered it, the more certain she became of her mother's blame being upon her head.

Aubrey knew that Marty was grown and made his own decisions, but the fact that Clara had not seen her son in years, with the next time being the last time she would see him, made Aubrey blame herself even more for his death. She kept thinking of things she could have done to prevent what happened, but she could come up with nothing. Her mind was whirling around in circles with each thought that crossed it.

Business was good at Esther's store. There weren't many times when Aubrey found herself standing with nothing to do. Even when the store found short breaks of hosting customers, Aubrey cleaned the floor over and over again. Boots kept tracking in dirty snow, but Aubrey didn't mind having to dispose of the mess with either a broom or mop. She was just thankful that there was always something to be done.

The day seemed to pass with more ease than Aubrey first figured, but she did not hear anything from her mama or papa. Through Esther's windows, Aubrey could see people walking to and fro through Moline, going about their everyday lives. Oh how she envied them, being able to take care of their business without worrying about being the cause of someone's death, and a loved one's for that matter.

Aubrey believed she would one day be in that carefree state of mind, and she knew that only God would be able to bring her there, but she feared how long it might take her. Putting all of her trust in the Lord was becoming more difficult it seemed, which she knew just shouldn't be.

To Esther's dread, Aubrey watched Rose Bennett walk into the store, with not so much as a sideways glance to them. When Rose walked, Aubrey noticed that she had a sort of arrogant demeanor. Her nose was slightly held up into the air, with one eyebrow held higher than the other, presenting a look of disdain for anyone she might pass.

Ever since she and Laura Woods were thrown in jail together by Deputy Kevin Johnson, Rose and Laura had not squabbled with each other, at least not in public.

"Well hello Ingrid!" Esther and Aubrey heard her shout.

Ingrid was a very short woman, but was a so-called "follower" of Rose Bennett. She was regarded as a follower because anytime Rose had a story to tell, or someone to gossip about, Ingrid was always right by her side, nodding her head in agreement that whatever it was Rose was saying held absolute truth.

Aubrey believed that Rose only used Ingrid, and treated her with any sort of regard because she would say and do just about anything Rose would tell her. There were one or two more women Rose could gossip to in town, and count on them to pass along her stories as well. Everything in the store was quiet at the moment, so Aubrey and Esther could hear almost everything Rose and Ingrid discussed while they stood behind the counter.

"Did you hear Rose? The Whittons are staying in town."

Rose gasped at this bit of juicy news, and at the mention of her last name, Aubrey listened more carefully to the women's conversation.

"Whatever for?" Rose asked, trying to sound quiet, but really not caring who overheard them.

Ingrid looked in Aubrey's direction, having noticed her behind the counter upon walking in the store, and whispered rather loudly, as if to attempt to shield their discussion but secretly hoping that Aubrey could hear, to let her know that she was beneath them.

"I haven't the slightest clue, but I do feel sorry for Clara. Poor dear, she needs our prayers."

Ingrid obviously believed that it was not a sin to gossip, as long as you promised to pray for them afterward, but the way she spoke of praying for Aubrey's mother made Aubrey see that Ingrid believed she was better than them. Rose nodded her head in agreement. She loved to be able to pray for other people and their pitiful states, but thought it shameful to have to be prayed for, as if that made one lesser of a person.

Aubrey's face burned with anger as she looked at Esther to see if she was hearing this. Esther returned her glance and shook her head from side to side.

"Your prayers, Ingrid, do not go past the ceiling," Aubrey thought to herself.

"Well, if you ask me, the whole thing was just a bad situation," Rose continued. "With one child kidnapping another. Then committing suicide! Those children must not have had the Christian raising we all thought. Either that, or Charles and Clara are being punished for something they are keeping hidden in their closet."

"Such a shame," Ingrid agreed, "I am sure it's a little bit of both."

Aubrey could not believe what she was hearing! How could anyone have such a disrespectful and judgmental view on another Christian brother and sister! And to talk about it in public! Aubrey was shaking in rage, doing all she could to keep herself calm. Esther could see Aubrey fighting for control of her body, so while the women kept shopping Esther grabbed Aubrey's hand and took her to the back room.

"Now Aubrey, I know you feel like fighting right now, but you've got to ignore what they say child."

"Ignore what they say! How can I ignore what they say?" Aubrey burst into sobs, being so hurt by the wretchedness of her fellow church members.

"Just keep yourself in check. Don't show them that they have control of your emotions. They are lower than grub worms child, and they are miserable people trying to make others around them miserable."

Esther hugged Aubrey and held her tightly for a moment while she cried. Esther had seen Rose and Ingrid do some pretty low things, but this was the nastiest of them all. Shortly the bell that sat on the counter, to alarm Esther of a customer, was rung. She took a deep breath and said,

"Do what you believe God would approve of, but wipe your tears. Don't let them see you've been crying."

Aubrey immediately began wiping her face, fanning herself with her hands to make the redness in her cheeks disappear while she sniffled. Esther went back into the store to help the ringing customers. Aubrey almost went back into the store, but decided that this would most probably not be wise.

She was not afraid to face them, but rather was afraid of losing control of her tongue, and possibly her fist, so Aubrey chose to stay in Esther's back room until Rose and Ingrid left. Her flesh wanted to go out there, look them both square in the eyes, and tell them that if they ever said another word about her and her family, then she would personally knock their teeth down their throats!

Her spirit however, kept telling her that doing that would be displeasing to God, sinking to their level, and allowing them to control her. Aubrey therefore stayed in the back room, not wanting to put herself in such a weakening position. Aubrey knew that God had heard every word said, and that He would repay them, but oh how she wanted so badly to take matters into her own hands!

At one point in time, Aubrey got down on her knees and prayed for God's strength to not try to get Rose and Ingrid back, and also praying for God to help her forgive them. Rage still seared through Aubrey, but had she given in to temptation and gave those "holier-than-thou" women a piece of her mind, then that would have just given them something else to talk about.

To be honest, Aubrey did not want to pray at all, but her raising, along with the knowledge she had of God and His word prevailed. She had to make herself pray and do the right thing, though sometimes doing the right thing means doing absolutely nothing at all, like in this particular situation.

Soon Aubrey heard the store's door slam shut, informing her that Rose and Ingrid must have left. Taking in a long deep breath, Aubrey turned the handle on the wooden door and stepped back into the store. Esther was writing some figures down on a piece of paper, and then looked up at Aubrey.

"You alright child?"

Aubrey sighed then replied, "Yes ma'am, but that was rough."

"I think you handled it splendidly child. You never know, that might have been God testing you." Aubrey hadn't even thought of that.

"Well, I barely passed I'll tell you that! If you hadn't been here, I probably would have made a fool of myself." Both women chuckled, with no one now being in the store to hear them.

"I don't know why they bother to go to church since they both think they are better than everyone in the church house, including the preacher!" Esther said. Aubrey laughed, starting to feel a little more at ease.

"Thanks Esther, you're a good friend."

"Child, I'm just human, but I try to keep in mind that humans ain't supposed to act like animals."

"If only Rose and Ingrid would adopt that concept," Aubrey thought, "then Moline would probably be a much better place."

As any normal person would do, Aubrey kept replaying the unpleasant conversation between Rose and Ingrid in her mind over and over again. She tried to make herself stop by thinking on other things, but her thoughts were carried back again to the judgmental statements previously made. The only break Aubrey received from them was when she helped a customer, or when she conversed with Esther. She tried not to show her pain, but Aubrey knew it was evident.

The day was drawing to a close with the sun slowly sinking in the West, so Aubrey thought she would get some fresh air by going back to the hotel. People still walked up and down the snow-covered streets, with some going in and out of buildings. Aubrey had heard the train pull through the station at different times during the day, but she paid little attention to its loud roaring, and ear-piercing whistle.

As Aubrey walked to the hotel she thought, "Before Marty found me on that train, my life made sense. After Breu rescued me, everything started getting back to normal, and now, I feel so broken and confused."

Without realizing it, this feeling of desolation was haunting Aubrey almost every second. Her mother, the main person of the few she could turn to, was in her own world of pain, and Aubrey, still being unsure as to whether or not Clara blamed her for Marty's death, was absolutely terrified to find out for certain where her mother's true feeling lie.

Aubrey counted on Charles, her papa, to be the mediator between the two of them. She could rely on him for news of how her mother was handling this great tragedy, and updates as to where they would be residing the next night. As Aubrey stepped inside the hotel, she tried to clear her mind for the reunion with her parents.

The hotel had a hardwood floor, and was now slippery from customers entering and leaving, tracking in snow, just as they had done at Esther's store all day. Aubrey could hear a low hum of voices coming from somewhere hidden, along with the desk clerk informing someone on available rooms.

Aubrey made her way to the room her mama and papa occupied, and gently knocked on the door. She became quite nervous, with her heart rate increasing due to the fear of her grieving mother answering the door. She hadn't seen Clara all day, and though her heart longed to see her mother, fear gripped Aubrey, like a lion's jaw grips his prey. Aubrey held her fear captive, because right now, she did not know how to let it go and put her faith in the Lord.

Footsteps were growing louder coming toward the door, then Aubrey took in a deep breath and held it in. It was Charles yet again who opened the door much to Aubrey's relief, but when he bid her enter their room, she was dismayed to see her grief-stricken, tiny built mother, rocking back and forth in the room's wooden rocking chair being in a daze, staring off into the distance, mentally not even existing in the room.

Knowing that it would be ridiculous to ask how they were doing, Aubrey instead asked, "Is there anything you need?"

"No, we're about to go down to Cat's Cafe to get something to eat. Care to join us?"

Aubrey thought a moment about her papa's offer, and hesitantly agreed to join them for supper. She was starving, and hoped that this feeling of awkwardness around her mother would fade away.

"I'll tell you what, you go on ahead of us and get us a seat, and we'll be on our way directly."

"Alright."

While heading out of the hotel, Aubrey figured that before she went into Cat's Cafe, she needed to let Esther know where she was going, so she would not get worried.

Chapter 4

"Supper"

A S AUBREY CROSSED the dirt and snow mixed street, a strong wind blew, piercing her body with icy air. The wind whipped so hard that it took Aubrey's breath away.

Trying not to feel sorry for herself Aubrey thought, "I'm beginning to wonder if I'll ever warm back up," but she didn't mean physically.

There was so much warmth in Esther's store that upon entering, Aubrey felt such relief. She planned on taking her time looking for Esther, so she could soak up as much warmth as she possibly could, but Aubrey was somewhat disappointed when Esther came into the store from the backroom.

"That didn't take long," Esther said.

"I'm going over to Cat's Cafe to eat with mama and papa. I wanted to tell you so you wouldn't worry. Would you like to join us?"

"Well thank you child, but I'd best stay here and look after the store. You go on ahead."

"Can you handle things until I get back?"

Esther began to laugh then replied, "Honey, I appreciate your concern, but I handled this store before you came, and Lord willing, I'll be handling it when you leave!"

Aubrey chuckled at Esther's strength and stamina, and then walked out of the store. As soon as Aubrey shut the store's door behind her she stopped, and looked down the street at the sheriff's office. A great sadness came over Aubrey as she thought about Breu, when it should have been happiness and comfort. Standing there, Aubrey pondered something that would bring her even more great sadness, but that she believed might be necessary.

Putting this horrid thought behind her for now, Aubrey went to Cat's Cafe. Charles and Clara arrived at the restaurant a few minutes after Aubrey did, with Clara barely raising her eyes from off of the floor until they came to the table.

The cafe was as noisy as ever, with the exception of the Whitton table being unusually quiet. As they began ordering their food, the waitress came over and Aubrey wondered what day it was. She had completely lost track of the week, which was not a custom with Aubrey.

"Excuse me ma'am, what is today?" she asked.

"It's Saturday," the waitress said, with a cheerful spirit.

"Oh," Aubrey softly replied, letting her eyes wander around the room. The waitress then walked away, leaving the family yet again in silence. Charles lightly played with his cloth napkin, as Clara sat there very still. Aubrey felt so awkward and uncomfortable. She had never felt this way with her parents before. It wasn't right! Aubrey was always able to talk to her mama and papa about anything, but now she was afraid to even speak a word to them. Despite her captive fears, Aubrey wanted so badly to hear them speak, so that maybe she could determine what their feelings toward her were, so Aubrey said,

"Tomorrow is Sunday. Are you both going to church?"

"Yes, we're going," Charles said with hesitation.

Clara did not even lift her eyes from the table. Aubrey hated to ask this next question, but she believed she had a right to know.

"So when are we going home?"

Charles pondered for a moment, and then replied, "I don't know Aubrey, but I'll let you know when we decide to go back. You can go back home anytime you want though."

"You know I can't do that," Aubrey said in almost a whisper.

Without even putting forth any sort of effort, Aubrey began to cry. She didn't make a sound, however tears freely poured down her cheeks. Would her life ever get back to normal? How long would she feel uncomfortable around her own folks? All of these questions, doubts, and fears ran rampantly through her unstill mind, but were blown away like autumn leaves in a strong breeze when Charles asked,

"Are you still planning on working for Doctor Starks?"

"Yes," Aubrey replied, as she thought seriously about Charles' question. "I'm just not sure when. I probably need to start soon though."

Their food was served shortly, but Charles, Clara, and Aubrey all ate in silence. Charles blessed the food, and asked for God's guidance through all of this difficulty and heartache. Quite frankly, that was the only thing any of them could do now.

Clara did not eat very much, but Charles ate her leftovers so as not to waste food. Aubrey herself didn't think she would be able to eat a lot either, but she surprised herself by eating just about everything on her plate. Each of them felt better physically, but emotionally, and even spiritually, at least on Aubrey's part, they were beaten down.

After eating, the Whittons did not stay long at the cafe. Aubrey said her goodbyes to Charles and Clara, promising that she would meet them at church in the morning. The walk back to Esther's store was an extremely cold one. It reminded her of how frozen she was in the saddle while she was Marty's captive.

God had helped her make it through that, and deep down, Aubrey believed God would help her overcome all of her fears, but right now, Aubrey could only see dark days ahead. There was no light at the end of this tunnel that Aubrey could visualize.

With the sun all but completely gone, a blue hue hovered over the town of Moline. Most of the stores were closing, but there were a few places in town that had lanterns lit on the inside so they could keep working. Aubrey could see that Mr. Hodges the blacksmith had his barn doors wide open, working on one last horse for the day changing the horse's shoes. The light that his lanterns threw off shined all the way to the other side of the street.

Aubrey figured that Esther had already closed for the day, which was really her secret hope, because Aubrey wanted only to sit down in front of the fire and read a book in silence, to try to get her mind off of the chaos her life seemed to be in.

What Aubrey really desired however, was to go home with her family. She longed so badly for her life to be the way it used to be, but Aubrey couldn't stop thinking that it was her fault as to why it changed. Aubrey would not let herself cry, but fought the tears, though they were like drops in a waterfall, ready to spill over the edge at any moment.

The one person who Aubrey naturally would have wanted to run to for comfort and love, but now strangely tried to avoid was Breu. She loved him so deeply, not wanting another, but Aubrey found herself hoping they would not cross paths. Aubrey hated herself for this, not completely understanding her actions, and feeling even more wretched because of it.

The last thing Aubrey wanted was for Breu to worry constantly about her and feel sorry for her, and Aubrey honestly did not know how long she could act like everything was going to be alright, because with her, it wasn't. She was having a hard enough time convincing herself that things would work out, much less try to make someone else believe it. So Aubrey thought it best if Breu did not see her in this pitiful state, but even she knew that this would not be able to last for very long.

Aubrey walked back into the store, thankful yet again for the warmth that immediately met her on the other side of the door. Esther was sweeping and singing a little tune as she worked. Esther's voice was like no others in town, and Aubrey loved to hear her talent, even if it was only a soft hum.

"How's your mama and papa child?"

"They seem to be doing alright. Mama hardly ate supper, but she never has been one to gorge herself."

Esther could see and hear the concern in Aubrey's face and voice, but she did not say anything about it.

"Is there anything you would like me to do?" Aubrey volunteered.

"No no, I'm just about done honey. You go get comfortable by the fire."

"I still don't know when we're going home. Are you sure you don't mind me staying here?"

"Child I've been enjoying your company. It gets lonely in here sometimes. You are welcome to stay here as long as you like. Don't you worry bout a thing."

This was a relief to Aubrey. She had no idea what she would have done if Esther wasn't there. Esther was like a second mother to Aubrey, and always had been. Aubrey grew up knowing Esther, being close to her all of the time ever since she could remember, and if Aubrey couldn't be with Clara, then with Esther she did want to be.

Aubrey went to Esther's room, kicked her boots off, grabbed a book from the small selection Esther owned in her shelf, and then sat down in the rocking chair next to the fire.

Sunday morning turned out to be a gloriously beautiful day. The sun shone blindingly bright, floating in a sky of pure blue with no clouds anywhere. Snow still lay atop the ground, trees, and buildings, making the atmosphere that much brighter.

Every year Aubrey enjoyed the snow and its purity, but this winter was obviously different. Aubrey was finding it more difficult with each passing day to enjoy much of anything. Fear and guilt clouded her heart, but Aubrey hoped that God would send a strong wind in this Sunday morning's sermon, to blow all of her pain away.

She stood there in front of Esther's aged looking mirror, staring into the glass as she buttoned her light pink coat. Aubrey wondered if her mother would be feeling better today, and if Clara would speak to her.

"My bible," Aubrey whispered to herself.

This was the first time she had even thought about it. She never forgot her bible, but the last time Aubrey had even seen it was the night of the suicide. Aubrey was reading her bible when Marty showed up at the Whitton's cabin. Suddenly her mind began going through the heart-wrenching events of that night, then Aubrey was quickly brought back to the present when Esther said,

"Are you ready child?"

Aubrey cleared her throat and replied, "Yes ma'am, but I don't have my bible. It's back at the cabin."

Esther walked over to her little bookshelf and pulled out a worn book. "Here," she said, "take this extra one. It's always good to keep more than one bible around."

Aubrey smiled as she took Esther's extra sword, holding it very cautiously because it looked as though it was about to fall apart. Together they made their way to the church, trying their best not to fall through any snow.

People were slowly gathering inside the white painted wooden building. As soon as Aubrey stepped inside, she began searching around the room with her eyes for the two people she expected to meet there. Clara and Charles had not arrived yet making Aubrey's heart sink when she figured this out.

Slowly, not trying to make eye contact with anyone, Aubrey walked to the bench her family always sat on. Just as Aubrey was about to take her seat, she happened to look across the room where stood Rose Bennett and Ingrid staring at her with their gossiping gazes. Aubrey's face began to burn with embarrassment and anger. She looked away from them, but each time she would glance in their direction she saw them still staring and talking, making it so obvious that Aubrey and the Whittons were the unfortunate subjects of their conversation.

So badly Aubrey wanted to stomp over to them and demand to know what their problem was, but Aubrey knew that would only start a ruckus which both gossiping women would thrive on. Aubrey couldn't give in to Rose and Ingrid's petty behavior, but what she couldn't understand was why they even bothered to attend church!

This made no sense at all to Aubrey, and she reminded herself that it was none of her business, however if Rose, Ingrid, or anyone kept talking about her family, Aubrey was unsure as to how long she could keep her own mouth shut and control her composure. Aubrey's thoughts were interrupted when a strong familiar voice said,

"Hello Aubrey."

Breu sat down on the bench, very close to Aubrey, letting his arm rest on the back of the bench around Aubrey's shoulders. Aubrey couldn't help but smile in his presence. She missed him, but something about their relationship kept haunting her.

"Hi Breu. You look well."

"I feel good, but it's you I'm concerned about."

This is what Aubrey didn't want. She didn't want Breu to see her pain, her doubts, or her fears, even though she knew that he was there to share them. Aubrey wanted to hold her fears captive, not allowing anyone to help carry her burden because as she still believed, she deserved this pain for being the cause of her own brother's death.

"I'm doing fine. Just trying to get use to Esther's bed," she insisted, trying to force a smile.

Now she was lying. How could she lie to Breu? Aubrey felt so rotten and terrible for telling Breu this lie, but without her knowing it, Breu did not believe a thing she just said. He could easily see through her poorly crafted mask. Aubrey's mouth said one thing, but her countenance and behavior completely said another, but since church was about to begin, Breu let it go for now, planning to hold a more intimate conversation with his wife to be later. He knew Aubrey wasn't a liar, but that she was trying to cover up her pain, for reasons he did not yet know or understand.

Just as services were about to begin, Charles and Clara walked in, hurriedly going to their seats. Aubrey was relieved to see her parents, but just as she had been dreading, Clara did not speak a word to Aubrey. There were times during the sermon when Aubrey thought she would have to leave so she could go cry. It was incredibly painful being so close to her mother, yet being very far away from her at the same time.

Breu could see that something was wrong with his fiancé, but until she admitted to it, he would not know what it was. What Aubrey didn't realize was that Breu was hurting too. Seeing Aubrey, and his dear friends Charles and Clara in pain and coming apart, made him feel so helpless and deeply concerned.

Aubrey wasn't hiding anything from him, though she thought she was, and he planned on getting to the bottom of things the first chance he got. Breu would have to pray, and figure out the best way to approach this matter without making Aubrey angry and pushing her away.

Service was over, and Aubrey honestly did not know what to do with herself. Breu walked her back to Esther's store, which was closed on Sunday, then had to get back to his office. Charles and Clara did not say much to anyone after church, but hastily went back to the hotel.

After eating a cold piece of ham, Aubrey thought of something she could do. "Esther, I'm going to go talk to Dr. Starks. I'll be back in a minute."

"Alright child, take your time."

Aubrey threw on her coat once more, and headed out of the door. "If I'm going to be stuck here in town, then I might as well get started doing what I came here to do," she thought.

She reached Dr. Starks' office, gently tapping on the door. Not hearing a sound, Aubrey walked inside and saw Dr. Starks sitting in his chair asleep. Aubrey quietly giggled at this comical sight, and then slammed the door behind her to wake him up.

Naturally the sound of the door slamming, and the bell loudly ringing startled Dr. Starks. He jumped, grumbled and groaned, then when his eyes focused, saw Aubrey standing at the door.

"Sleeping on the job?" Aubrey said teasingly.

"Aubrey! How are you dear?"

"I'm fine doctor. I actually came by to ask about working for you."

"Yes yes," he said standing to his feet as he grunted.

"I was wondering if I could start working tomorrow."

Dr. Starks raised his eyebrows and then replied, "Why you can start anytime you'd like, but uh, are you sure you are ready?"

Aubrey hesitated but said, "Yes. I am ready."

"Alright then, be here at seven o' clock tomorrow morning."

"Thank you doctor," Aubrey stated gratefully.

"Oh Aubrey, how are your mother and father doing?"

Aubrey had to choose her words carefully, because to be honest, she did not know. Her mother did not speak to her, and her papa was so concerned with her mother that he did not say much at all. After hastily coming up with something to reply, Aubrey spoke.

"They are still having a difficult time as you can imagine, but they are trying to make it through."

Doctor Starks nodded his head, being a little disappointed that Aubrey hadn't gone into much detail, but knowing that she was hurting too, he did not pry further.

"Here, take this to them. If they are having any trouble sleeping, this will help," he said as he walked over to his medicine cabinet.

"Oh but, I don't have any money."

Dr. Starks chuckled and replied, "It's on the house." Aubrey took the glass bottle of medicine, and smiled.

"Thank you again Dr. Starks."

"So I'll see you at seven then?" he reminded.

"Yes sir. I'll see you at seven."

Aubrey then left the doctor's office, feeling a new anxiousness with beginning a job in the morning, a new routine, and a change. Before returning to Esther's store, she wanted to stop by the hotel, to give her parents the bottle of medicine. Inside the hotel room however, a completely different conversation was taking place.

"Do you think you feel like going home today?" Charles asked his wife who sat in the chair looking out over the town through the window. She sighed.

"I know you're tired of this hotel room Charles, I am too, but I can't go back."

Charles could not believe what he just heard! Can't go back? How could Clara not go back to their home, the place they raised their children, where they had so many things and memories? Charles tried not to show his shock, but kept his voice calm and reasonable when he said,

"What do you mean you can't go back? We have to go back home Clara."

"Believe me when I say that I do want to be back home. I long to be back in my cabin, close to my things, close to Marty." She paused for a moment, and then continued.

"I can't live in that cabin with Mar . . . ," she had to catch her breath for the excruciatingly painful thing she was about to attempt to say. She took in a deep breath, trying not to lose control with tears already gushing out of her eyes. "With Marty's blood on the floor," Clara was finally able to get out. "If I try, I'll go crazy Charles, I just can't do it. Even covering it with a rug doesn't help."

Charles then realized that her mind was made up, but for some strange reason, he did not want to argue the point with her, which was unlike him. Truthfully, Charles didn't think he could stand being in that cabin any worse than Clara. Marty was his son too, and seeing his blood on the floor made Charles get sick to his stomach. He had thought that when he asked her this question, if they went home, they could just ignore the blood-stained floor and get their lives back in order. However, Clara made up all of their minds on this issue, and Charles did not want to fight over it.

This meant that there was only one thing to do, and Charles was going to keep this secret to himself. Their discussion ended when Charles and Clara heard a tapping on the door. Charles was certain that it was Aubrey on the other side, and his certainty was assured when he opened it and Aubrey stood there.

Not needing an invitation, Aubrey walked into the hotel room. She saw Clara sitting down, looking out through the window, but she did not turn to look at Aubrey. Instead, Clara kept gazing through the dirty glass, lost in deep thought.

"Doctor Starks sent over this medicine," Aubrey said as she handed Charles the glass bottle. "He said that if you couldn't sleep to take this, and it would help."

"Thank you," Charles replied, setting the clear bottle on the small round wooden table the hotel room owned.

"I'm going to start working for him tomorrow morning at seven," she said, hoping to hear some sort of happiness from her parents.

"Good," Charles replied without even smiling. "That will be good for you."

"Yes," she stated bluntly, being very disappointed.

Charles knew his daughter wondered when they would be going home, but he was not about to tell her anything of the previous conversation he and her other just held, nor of what he was planning, because he knew that it would only upset her further.

"Well is there anything you need before I go back to Esther's?"

"No I don't believe."

"Alright, well I love you both."

"We love you too."

Aubrey looked one more time at her mother, who never once acknowledged her and never said a word, to see if she would return Aubrey's affectionate statement, but Clara said nothing. This broke Aubrey's heart. Now Aubrey was certain that her mother blamed her for Marty's death. She wanted to run away and cry. Without saying another word, Aubrey left.

She couldn't stop the tears that freely fell down her cheeks. Aubrey kept wiping them away so Esther would not see that she had been crying when she came into the store. There was only one thing Aubrey wanted to do, and that was to find Esther's worn out bible, sit down by the fire, and start reading.

So many times Aubrey found strength, peace, and comfort from God's word. That's what she needed right now, especially since she couldn't seem to receive any of these things from her parents.

Entering into Esther's room, Aubrey took off her coat, grabbed Esther's bible, and then sat down by the fire. When she opened the cover of the holy book, the name Henry Worthington popped out at Aubrey in big cursive letters.

"Hmm," Aubrey thought, "this must either be someone very important, or the previous owner of this old bible."

Aubrey couldn't stop staring at the name. It seemed to sound familiar, but Aubrey could not pinpoint where she might have heard it from.

Finally, she turned to the book of Psalm, and began reading in the thirty-seventh chapter. Out of all of the chapters Aubrey had read in the bible so far, this particular one was her favorite. Aubrey read and read, but curiosity was getting the best of her because of the large name on the inside of the cover. Esther sat across from Aubrey in another chair knitting, but stopped when Aubrey asked,

"Esther, who is Henry Worthington?"

Esther wasn't sure of what to say, for fear of saying the wrong thing, but carefully replied, "He was a slave owner. I was one of his slaves."

That was all Esther said about this subject for now, and Aubrey could tell that there was something Esther did not want brought out into the open. Aubrey wanted to ask more questions, because Esther's blunt answer only fueled Aubrey's curiosity, but she respected Esther, and did not want to upset her, especially since Esther was the only person with whom she could stay. There was one question however which outweighed the others.

"If this Henry Worthington was Esther's slave owner, then why does she have his bible?" she couldn't stop wondering.

For the present though, Aubrey would have to let her curiosity burn out, but it was very difficult. Twilight was approaching, and Aubrey had grown tired of reading, so she put on her coat and told Esther that she was going for a little stroll to get some fresh air before dark. As Aubrey strolled along the porches of town, her eye glimpsed something that she had to look twice at to even believe. Aubrey's mouth dropped open, and she nearly stumbled over her own feet because of this sight.

Hiding in the almost complete dark between two buildings, were Ethan Bennett and Tonya Woods! These were the eldest children of Rose Bennett and Laura Woods. Ethan was now the age of eighteen, while Tonya was seventeen. Tonya had long blonde hair, as straight as a board, and she was very lean. Ethan was a strapping young man, with the strength to help any one with any task necessary.

Aubrey saw the two standing close to each other, and Ethan at times, stroked Tonya's stringy blonde hair. Aubrey couldn't believe her own eyes! Despite the dark night closing in around them, Aubrey could easily see that there was an intimate relationship between the two.

"If their mothers knew!" Aubrey thought shivering at the idea of what a fight there would be if Rose and Laura found out about their children's secret love!

Then Aubrey saw Ethan kiss Tonya, and this confirmed her assumptions about them. Ethan must have felt eyes staring at him, because after the kiss he looked in Aubrey's direction, catching her glare. Aubrey quickly turned her head forward, but realized that she was only kidding herself. Slowly Aubrey looked back at where the couple stood, and she noticed that Tonya had already gone, but Ethan was now staring her down, with anger and embarrassment on his countenance.

With the reaction Ethan was giving Aubrey, she quickly decided that she would cut her stroll even shorter than what it originally was. She didn't feel like being confronted by him. She went a little further, so as not to make it obvious that she had seen them and was now trying to avoid Ethan. Aubrey soon turned around and headed back to Esther's store, wishing now that she had never left.

Chapter 5

"Gazebo"

THE NEXT MORNING, Aubrey was walking to Dr. Starks' office, ready to work and get her mind off of Marty's death, her grieving folks, and the guilt of blaming herself for Marty's suicide. She left early because Aubrey got tired of waiting around for seven o' clock. Aubrey was sure Dr. Starks wouldn't mind anyway.

When she arrived at the doctor's office, Aubrey knocked, but just like last time heard no sound. Checking to see if the door was locked, Aubrey softly turned the handle and was able to go on in. The doctor was nowhere to be seen, with no lantern even being lit anywhere.

"Hmm," she thought, "this is peculiar."

"Dr. Starks," Aubrey said loudly. She waited, but heard no sound. "Dr. Starks," she repeated a few times more, but louder. Finally, Aubrey heard someone rummaging about in one of the back rooms.

"Just a minute," Dr. Starks shouted back, so after hearing the sound of his voice Aubrey took her coat off, and began looking for something to light the lanterns with.

"Aubrey dear!" Dr. Starks loudly said with enthusiasm a few moments later. "You are early," he finished looking at his pocket watch.

"Good morning doctor. I apologize for being here early, but I couldn't wait to get started. Were you asleep?"

"My old bones seem to want more rest now than in my younger days, but I'm glad you're early. There are things I need to show you before we begin the day."

"Alright doctor but first, where are your matches?"

Breu was awake early as well this beautiful Monday morning. He waited for Kevin, his deputy, to arrive. Breu had some business to discuss with a Mr. Logan Benton, about a very large amount of land with a certain gazebo on it. He planned to buy it and surprise Aubrey with the news. "Maybe," Breu thought, "this will cheer her up."

Kevin arrived at his usual time, and when he walked into the jailhouse he announced some good news of his own.

"Ella and I are expecting another child."

"Really? Well congratulations!" Breu said, slapping Kevin on the back. Kevin laughed at Breu's excitement, and then they both shook hands.

"Is Ella excited?" Breu asked.

"Very excited. She loves children, especially babies."

"Well that's a good thing considering that you now have three!"

Both men laughed, then Breu put on his jacket and bid Kevin goodbye for a few hours. Breu was extremely happy for Kevin and Ella, and then the thought crossed his mind about maybe him and Aubrey one day having children. He had never thought about having children, but ever since he met Aubrey his mind and heart were going to places they had never been before, like being a husband.

Breu had always pictured himself a loner, an independent free-spirit, but he did long for a mate, and he truly believed that Aubrey was not only who he wanted, but who he needed. He was certain that God brought them together for a reason, and Breu intended on seeing it through.

Now that he and Aubrey were engaged, Breu wanted to buy Mr. Logan Benton's land since Aubrey loved it so much, and then begin building a house for them to live in. At least, this was his plan for the moment. It took a little while to get to Mr. Benton's place, but Breu was finally there and willing to pay a decent price for the land.

The house that Logan lived in looked to Breu like it must have been something in its hay day, but now it was just an old worn down shack. The steps creaked very loudly when Breu stepped upon them, and he made sure that he stepped lightly and cautiously, for fear of falling through.

The porch was no different, but when Breu made his way to the screened door, before he was even able to knock Mr. Benton said, "Who's there?" Breu figured that Logan could tell when someone was there, because of all the noise that was rendered upon walking to the door.

"Sheriff Breu Lawrence," he replied.

Breu heard faint footsteps coming to the door. Mr. Benton and Breu had never met before, but that was about to change. The door, just like the steps and porch, squeaked when Mr. Benton opened it, then a tall lanky gray-haired elderly gentleman stepped into the light. Before inviting Breu inside he studied the star Breu wore on his shirt, to make sure Breu really was who he said he was. After a few moments Mr. Benton said,

"Sheriff huh?"

"Yes sir," Breu answered. "I was hoping I could speak with you for a moment sir."

"Come on in son."

Breu entered the shack, thankful to be out of the cold, and to see a fire blazing in the fireplace.

"Have a seat son," Mr. Benton commanded. "How about a hot cup of coffee?"

"That sounds mighty fine," Breu replied with a smile.

Mr. Benton left the main room to go start some coffee, so Breu stood by the fire to get warm before he began their conversation. After a while, when Logan came back into the room where Breu stood by the fire, Breu noticed that this man was very elderly indeed. He sort of dragged his feet as he walked and took short steps. Breu imagined that Logan did this, regardless of whether he could walk well or not, because with how tall this man was, if he did fall something would most likely break.

Logan was bringing Breu a cup of steaming coffee, which Breu accepted gladly. Then both men sat back down on the, just as Breu figured, creaky old furniture, immediately taking sips of their coffee.

"Well Sheriff Lawrence, it's nice to finally meet you. Forgive me for not making your acquaintance sooner, but as you might have guessed, I don't leave my cabin much."

"I completely understand, but please, call me Breu."

"Alright Breu, what's on your mind?"

Breu took another sip of his coffee and then began, "I am looking into buying a good piece of land to begin building a house on. My fiancé and I were both wondering about the piece of land you own where the gazebo sits."

"Ah," he said. "The gazebo."

Breu watched Logan's facial expressions, and after mentioning the gazebo, he seemed to be taken back to the past in a deep trance.

"Yes," Breu carefully continued. "I actually brought her to the gazebo to propose. She was quite taken with the beautiful landscape, as was I, then when I looked into the land records your name was discovered."

"I see," Logan said. A heavy sigh came from him, which made Breu believe that he did not want to sale.

"I do not want to pressure you into selling if you wish not to. You seem to have a great attachment to this place."

"No no. I will sale." He paused for a moment. "I knew this day would come." Breu was quite confused by his actions and statements.

"I am willing to pay whatever price you have in mind."

Mr. Benton sat there in silence for a few minutes, making Breu wonder if he was thinking, or reliving something from the past.

"I'll make you a deal. I will sell you this property, and the property where the gazebo is, for half of the price that it's worth, if you will allow me to finish out my days here in my cabin."

Breu was shocked at Mr. Benton's offer. He raised his eyebrow, but could not seem to speak.

"You seem like a decent presentable fellow, so I would be happy for my land to be in your hands."

"A-are you sure?" Breu asked wanting to be certain he had heard Mr. Benton correctly.

"Of course."

"Alright. It's a deal."

Breu stood up to shake hands with Logan and then sat back down again because Logan looked as though he had more to say.

"I want to give you a little history on this land you are about to buy." Breu sipped the last of his coffee, and then sat back in the chair he was occupying.

"My wife and I fell in love with this place, just as you described of you and your fiancé. I built this cabin, then the gazebo. Hannah loved her gazebo. If ever I couldn't find her, I could always go to the gazebo and she would be there. She longed to have children, but the Lord saw fit not to bless us with any.

We were so in love, with a bright future ahead of us. Then the war began. Hannah begged me not to go, and I didn't want to, but soldiers rode through town looking for any able bodies. I couldn't refuse to do anything, so I joined the confederacy, not knowing where I was going, or if I'd ever be back.

Hannah cried at some point everyday until I left. She was so heartbroken, but I went off to war. Two years later, the war was still raging on, and I was shot in the leg. I've never been able to walk well ever since. I was relieved of my duties, and sent back home."

Mr. Benton stopped for a moment, and sighed again. Breu could see pain in his eyes.

"When I came home, I looked everywhere for Hannah. There was no sign of her anywhere. There was still one place I could go look, but when I got to the gazebo, it was empty and bare. I couldn't understand what was going on, but then I saw it. A small wooden cross planted in the ground on the right side of the gazebo.

I couldn't believe my eyes when I read, "Hannah Benton, died June 1, 1863." I frantically rode into town to get some answers from someone, probably because I just couldn't believe it. I found out that she died from smallpox. Hannah died three months before I came home, but she requested before she passed, that she would be buried next to her precious gazebo.

I haven't shared this with anyone before, until now. I just wanted you to know what this place really means to me, and that I want you to take good care of it."

"I will," Breu replied, having to clear his throat. He was almost brought to tears because of Mr. Benton's story.

"I have one more request before I will let you have my land, and that is to bury me beside my beloved wife when I die."

"It will be done. I give you my word."

Breu stood to his feet one more time, shook Mr. Benton's hand, then both men bid the other goodbye. Excitement was soaring through Breu as he got on his horse and left. He couldn't wait to tell Aubrey the good news. Breu knew just how he would let her know. As he rode back into town Breu's mind was racing, trying to form a plan.

Breu decided that he would take Aubrey back out to the gazebo, and just as he had proposed, let her know that soon all of this beautiful countryside would be hers. It took restraint against himself not to go on ahead and tell her, but Breu wanted everything to be romantic and perfect.

Logan still sat in his chair back at the old shack. Except for the sounds of fire crackling, everything was silent. Mr. Benton stared deep into the fire that burned, but his vision was stuck in a memory. The memory of his faithful, devoted wife, the love that they shared, and the abandonment she suffered which he deemed necessary to serve his country.

The memory that still outshone all the others, the one freshest on his mind, was the last day he ever saw his precious love again. The day he left her standing on the porch of their once beautiful home, professing her love to him as she nearly drowned herself in tears.

This was the strongest memory Logan had of Hannah, and one he wished he could forget. Many times after the discovery of her death Logan had considered suicide, to relieve his heart of the guilt he felt for leaving her at all. He knew he could not have prevented Hannah's death, but at least he could have been there with her as she passed.

The day he found out about his wife's departure, was the day that Logan Benton inwardly died. His heart still beat, his body still moved, his lungs still breathed, but Logan was dead. After that he never desired to go anywhere, or do anything, because his beloved was not there with him sharing his experiences.

Logan was forty-eight when he went off to war, and in his mind that was the age of his death, because never again would he see his sweet Hannah again.

He did not go into detail with Breu, about how he felt the day he came back from war, but Logan believed he had shared enough to make Breu understand how important this place was to him. Logan could tell what kind of person you were, just by spending a small amount of time with you, and he determined that Breu was the man he would want his land going to when he died.

Mr. Benton sat there in a long daydream of his past, just like so many years before, not knowing why God was keeping him alive when he longed to be with his beloved. Logan did not question the Almighty, but like so many people, simply couldn't understand His ways.

As long as he could stay in his old shack for the rest of his life to be near his sweet Hannah, Logan would be content. He believed Breu would keep his word, but whether he did nor didn't, Mr. Logan Benton was an old soldier, and he wasn't going anywhere.

Breu was now back in town, full of the anticipation of him soon owning his own land. The faster he could build a house, the faster he could have Aubrey as his wife. Breu wasn't trying to rush the process, but he could see his future clearly ahead of him, and Breu was anxious to begin spending the rest of his life with his true love.

The morning passed, with the afternoon now being the time of day. Dr. Starks' office had not been busy, leaving him plenty of time to go over everything with Aubrey. She was a quick learner, and whenever a patient would come in, she would have Dr. Starks the things he needed in no time.

He was quite enjoying her being there working for him. Though they weren't busy with patients, Dr. Starks could easily tell that Aubrey would be an asset, making tasks a lot faster and better for him to accomplish. Aubrey was feeling a great satisfaction in working as a nurse already. Her responsibilities did not take away her pain, only God could do that, but staying busy kept her mind off of her guilt.

Most of the day was spent learning. Aubrey had studied all of the medicines Dr. Starks kept in his medicine cabinet, so she had a familiarity with the things he showed her already. Aubrey was excited about working for Dr. Starks, but soon the working day had come to an end.

"So I'll see you at seven in the morning?" Aubrey asked the doctor as she put on her coat.

"I'll be here," he confirmed with a smile.

Aubrey walked out of the office, immediately tensing her muscles because of the cold. The earth again had a dusky blue hue being reflected off of the snow. She thought, as she began walking, that maybe things would start getting better.

Before going back to Esther's, Aubrey wanted to check on her parents. She had not seen them all day, having barely seen them the day before. Quickly Aubrey made her way to the hotel because she was freezing. This time however, when she knocked on the door, instead of Charles answering, it was her mother's faint "come in" that she heard.

Aubrey did not see Charles anywhere in the room. Clara sat in the chair, sewing patches of cloth on some of Charles' holey pants.

"Hello dear," Clara said, never looking up from her work.

"Hello mama. How are you today?"

Aubrey was really afraid to say too much to Clara, for the fear of Clara's blame being somehow confirmed, on Aubrey.

"I'm making it dear. How are you?"

Aubrey was so deafened by her fear and guilt, that she could not even hear the love in Clara's voice.

"Alright. I started working for Dr. Starks today."

"Oh. How was it?"

"It was fine. We spent most of the day going over things."

Clara then became silent, making Aubrey even more afraid.

"Where is papa?"

"He has been at the cabin today. He brought me my sewing material so I would have something to do."

This told Aubrey that her mother had no intentions of going back home any time soon, but she was unaware of the conversation her folks had about this previously.

"He should be getting back anytime now."

Aubrey felt too uncomfortable with staying a long time near her mother, but she longed to see her papa as well. Finally she said,

"Is there anything you need before I go?"

"No. I think we're fine."

"Alright. I'll be back tomorrow sometime."

Clara didn't say another word. Aubrey took that as her goodbye, then left.

This was the first time Clara had spoke to Aubrey since Marty's suicide. She felt comfort at first since her mother talked to her, but Clara's words were not enough to drown her silence, therefore Aubrey still felt blame for her brother's death.

Before Aubrey got to the door of Esther's store, she felt a hand on her shoulder swinging her around. She thought at first that it was Breu but he was too aggressive to be Breu, and he did not have Breu's face.

"Hey! What are you doing?" she demanded fiercely.

"You saw didn't you?" Ethan Bennett asked with anger in his voice.

"Saw what?"

"You saw me and Tonya. I know you did. Admit it!"

"Ethan Bennett, you had better calm down before I make you regret touching my shoulder!"

Aubrey was furious now with the way Ethan had touched and talked to her. She was willing to fight, even a man who was twice her size. Aubrey had already been through this before.

"You don't just come swinging people around demanding an admission to something Ethan. You acted like an animal. That was extremely unnecessary and not the way someone of your age should behave."

Aubrey realized that she sounded like a school teacher, but she didn't even slightly care. She refused to be treated in that manner by anyone.

"Did you see us?"

"Ethan, I am not going to answer you if you insist on being brutish!" Ethan let out a heavy sigh of impatience.

"Please tell me if you saw us," he said more calmly.

"I did see you."

"Have you said anything about it?"

"No I haven't, and I will not. It's none of my business. But you might want to be more careful, because if I saw the two of you, then someone else is likely to, and they won't keep their mouth shut as I have."

A look of relief came over Ethan. Though he was eighteen years old, Ethan could be quite intimidating by his size, but this did not work with Aubrey.

Breu was far down the street, but saw Ethan swing Aubrey around by her shoulder. He had been running to come and defend her, but when he got to them, their conversation had ended. He was angry by what he saw, and ready to take Ethan to jail for being violent with his wife to be.

"What's going on here?" Breu demanded when he finally got between the two.

"Nothing Breu, Ethan was just leaving."

Ethan had a look on his face, telling Breu that he was willing to fight but he slowly backed off, yet before he walked away Breu said with great intensity,

"I'd better not ever see you lay a finger on her, or any woman like that again."

Ethan did not say anything, but stared Breu down, and then finally he walked away.

"What was that all about?" he asked Aubrey, grabbing her hand.

"I saw him and Tonya Woods sharing their affection to each other between those two buildings over there yesterday. He saw me looking at them, and wanted to know if I told anyone."

"He better be glad I was down the street when he touched you like that, or he wouldn't have any teeth."

"I'm alright Breu."

"Well, I've got to get back. I was in the middle of some business that needed tending to, but I want to spend time with you. Don't make any plans for tomorrow evening. I want to take you somewhere. Make sure you bundle up."

Before Aubrey could say anything, Breu kissed her on the lips and was gone. Aubrey told herself that she had better get to Esther's before anything else happened.

Charles eventually came back to the hotel. He breathed heavily from having worked out at their cabin, being chilled to the bone. Night was upon them, with all of the stores and businesses being closed for what remained of the day. When Charles got into the hotel room, he kicked his boots off, sighed heavily, and climbed in the bed beside his wife who had already fallen asleep. He did not change his clothes however, because on this night, Charles knew he would most probably be up again soon.

The town of Moline fell asleep, in the same routine it always did. Everything was cold, dark, and quiet. Aubrey and Esther were sleeping soundly, only dreaming of what the next day would hold, until Aubrey's turned into a nightmare. Esther was quickly brought back to consciousness when she began hearing a faint commotion outside. Someone walking along the street late at night thought he saw smoke rising into the sky.

Had it not been for the light from the moon, and no clouds in the sky, then the smoke would surely have gone unnoticed, however, when it was brought to someone's attention, he hastily ran to the jailhouse to inform Sheriff Breu Lawrence.

Breu stepped outside to see what held the man's concern, and after widening his eyes somewhat, he saw the smoke as well. Studying the smoke and its rising stream, he was able to determine that the woods were not on fire, but the smoke seemed to be getting thicker.

The surroundings were too blackened by the night for Breu to see anything more, but the longer he stood there watching the smoke rise to the sky, the more he became concerned. The direction that the smoke rose from was the same direction the Whitton's cabin was in.

Breu thanked the man for having a quick eye, but told him to hang around the jail until he got back, just in case he needed him. He jumped onto his horse's back, and then galloped in the direction of the smoke.

As Breu got closer to Charles and Clara's cabin, the smell of smoke became stronger. Each time his horse's hooves pounded the ground while he galloped, Breu felt his heart beat through his chest with anxiousness. Finally being near the cabin, Breu's fear became reality when he saw a blazing fire through the trees. The cabin was on fire!

Chapter 6

"Fire!"

B REU DID NOT leave his horse's back, but frantically went back and forth on his horse in a pace, trying to see how bad the fire actually was. The whole cabin was engulfed in flames, and Breu could not fight it himself, but he feared with the way the fire was raging, that fighting the fire would do no good period. He turned his horse and galloped back to town.

"How could this have happened?" he thought. "There was no storm, so lightning shouldn't have caused it. Surely someone did not start the fire," he reasoned within himself.

Breu's horse galloped as fast as he physically could, with Breu still pushing him to go faster. Breu was not only concerned about the Whitton cabin, because that was his fiancé's home, but also because the Whitton's were his dear friends. He was like a son to them before he even met Aubrey, and he allowed them to take the place of his deceased parents. Arriving in town, Breu shouted at the man who brought the smoke to his attention to begin with.

"The Whitton cabin is on fire! Gather some men!"

Without answering, the man began to search through the town for able men willing to fight a fire. This was the commotion that woke Esther, and she was about to find out what on earth was going on. Moving quietly, so as not to awaken Aubrey, Esther made her way through the store and stepped outside in her robe. By now, a few men were on their horses ready to go fight the fire, waiting on orders from Sheriff Breu.

"What's the matter?" she asked one of them.

"Whitton's cabin is on fire. It's covered in flames."

Esther's jaw dropped as she covered her mouth and whispered, "Oh no!"

Esther went back inside to get dressed and go to Clara. Breu had arrived at the hotel and hurriedly ran to Charles and Clara's room, beating on the door. It took a few moments, but finally Charles came and opened the door.

"Charles, your cabin is on fire. Hurry up. I've got some men waiting to go."

"I know it's on fire."

This startled Breu. He became confused.

"What?"

"I know it's on fire Breu. I'm the one who set it."

Breu could not believe what he was hearing. He couldn't even speak from being so confused and caught off guard.

"Come in Breu, and I'll explain everything."

Breu was beginning to be agitated at Charles with his calmness about the situation when his own house was burning to the ground, but he stepped inside.

"Where's Breu?" one of the men who was waiting outside asked.

"I don't know, but we'd better get going or there won't be anything left." There were five men who rode to the Whitton cabin together to go fight the fire. Shortly after arriving however, the men saw that it was a lost cause. They could see that the house had been burning for a while now, and was completely unsalvageable.

"Let's go back boys," the eldest of the five said. "We'll just tell Sheriff Breu that we were too late."

Esther was walking as fast as she could to the hotel. Her legs would not permit her to run, which is what she would have done were she younger. She left Aubrey in her bed asleep, and was now beating on Charles and Clara's hotel room door. Charles let her in, not only the room, but also the conversation he and Breu were having. Clara was awake now, so the four discussed what was happening.

Charles and Clara explained everything to Breu and Esther thoroughly, leaving them both in shock. After hearing everything that was said, Breu's only concern was Aubrey. He was beginning to wonder what Charles was thinking, or rather, who didn't seem to think about Aubrey. Who was going to tell her that her father just burned their house to the ground?

Breu wasn't sure if Charles had noticed Aubrey's pain, and to do this would only add to her burdens. Breu believed that Charles and Clara should have thought this through a little more, for Aubrey's sake, but he did not let this thought slip out of his lips. He dreaded the moment when Aubrey would find out that her childhood home was gone.

Esther didn't have much to say, but sat there listening. She understood the pain her friends were going through, because she lost someone very dear to her a long time ago, but what was done was done, and there was no turning back now.

"What are you going to tell people Charles?" she asked.

"I'll just tell them that we needed a change, if I decide to tell anyone anything at all. I don't answer to anybody in this town beside the law."

"What do we tell them?" Breu asked.

"Tell them to mind their own business, and if they can't, to come ask me."

Charles was very grave when he made this statement, and everyone in the room knew he meant it.

"Aubrey is going to expect an explanation," Breu continued.

"You just tell her to come see me, and I'll explain everything."

Breu let out a heavy sigh, and stood realizing that there was nothing more to be done.

"Not only as your sheriff, but also as your friend and future son-in-law, if you plan to do anything drastic like this again, then let me know about it."

Breu was upset about all of this, and that was all he said before leaving the hotel room, but he made sure Charles heard the irritation, anger, and disappointment in his voice when he made his statement.

Charles could see that Breu was angry with what he did, but Charles couldn't help the way Breu felt, because he had to do what he had to do. Charles had to get his family back together, had to get them a good place to live, and had to get their lives back in order. He couldn't live in the hotel, and was about to lose his mind being stuck in it.

Esther sighed as well, standing to her feet to go. She gave Clara a tight hug, assured her friends that all would be alright, then left the hotel to go back to bed. The men who went to fight the fire all headed back home to their beds as well, figuring that Breu would want to know where they went.

Too many people were asleep for there to be a crowd stirred from all of the commotion, but Breu, Esther, Charles, and Clara prepared themselves for talk that would be going around the next morning. Breu sat down at his desk, shaking his head at what the night held. Esther was able to slip back in bed without waking Aubrey, but like Breu, dreaded the moment when Aubrey would find out about the cabin. Esther didn't see a sense in telling her guest about the fire, because Aubrey needed her rest, and what good would waking and fretting her at this hour do?

Since Esther was who Aubrey stayed with, Esther wasn't sure if she should break the news to Aubrey, or tell her that her papa has something to discuss with her. Esther did some praying before she fell asleep, and thought about what tomorrow would hold.

Esther's mind would not let her fall sleep immediately, but when she finally did, the morning seemed to come all too soon. She got out of bed at the usual time, but let Aubrey stay and sleep a couple of more hours. Esther caught herself shaking her head, still in disbelief at what Charles had done. Esther dressed, and began opening the store because customers would be entering soon.

Aubrey awoke, earlier than most mornings, from the sounds of people in the store. Falling back asleep would be nearly impossible, so Aubrey decided to go ahead and get ready to start a new day. Once dressed, she came into the store to see if she could help Esther with anything, because she had half an hour to spare. She looked around for Esther, but couldn't see her.

"Maybe she's at the back of the store helping someone," Aubrey thought.

A customer came to the counter, and since Esther wasn't in view, Aubrey took her place.

"How can I help you?" Aubrey asked the timid woman who handed her a short list. "I'll get these for you. Be right back."

As Aubrey gathered the supplies that were listed, she heard people talking about some incident that happened in the night, but she couldn't understand who they were talking about, or where it happened. She didn't even know what the incident was.

Having finished with the list, Aubrey came back to the counter.

"That will be two dollars and fifteen cents."

Without saying a word, the woman handed her the money, took the items she purchased and said, "I'm sorry."

This surprised Aubrey, but before she could say anything, the woman left the store.

"Sorry for what?" Aubrey said to herself. "Why on earth would she apologize to me like that?"

Aubrey couldn't stop thinking. Then, without being accompanied by an explanation, Aubrey had the strange sense that something was wrong. After having this feeling hit her, she began to notice people whispering and glancing her way. Now she felt uncomfortable.

"What's going on?" she screamed inside her mind.

"Oh, your awake child," Esther stated as she too got behind the counter.

Aubrey could see a look of worry on Esther's face.

"Esther, is something going on? Because a woman just apologized to me for something that I have no idea . . ."

"You need to go see your papa," Esther bluntly replied, interrupting Aubrey's sentence.

"Why do I need to see . . . ?"

"Just go talk to him Aubrey. There's something he needs to tell you child."

Again Esther cut off Aubrey's sentence, which she never did unless something serious was going on. Esther's words scared Aubrey, as did her grave tone and countenance. Aubrey left the counter to go put on her coat. She didn't know what was happening, but the only way she could know was to find Charles.

After Aubrey put on her coat and got to the hotel she knocked on the door, but no one answered. She waited a few more moments and knocked again, but there was still no answer. There wasn't even the sound of footsteps to be heard. Aubrey was becoming aggravated and impatient. Hastily she left the hotel and began asking those who passed by if they had seen Charles Whitton.

"I just saw him at the hardware store," one man answered, so Aubrey went.

The man was right, because upon entering the hardware store, Aubrey saw her papa standing inside talking to Wayne Haley, the owner of the store. Quickly she walked and got by his side, waiting for their conversation to end because she was raised not to interrupt. Aubrey crossed her arms with anxiousness, and sighed heavily more than once. Charles saw her walk up beside him though he was in the middle of a discussion, but did not look at her until the conversation was over. He knew why she was here, but at the moment, was unsure however if she knew yet about the cabin.

"Hello Aubrey," Charles said as he began walking out of the hardware store.

Aubrey stayed right beside him, not about to let him get away.

"I went to the hotel, but nobody answered. Where's mama?"

"Uh, she's in the meadow. She wanted to stay at the grave."

Aubrey noticed that Charles did not say his son's name, but only bluntly referred to Marty's burial ground as, "the grave." She didn't know if

Charles was that far removed from Marty, or if there was pain he felt, but kept hidden.

"What's going on? Esther said that you had something you needed to tell me, and why is everyone acting so strange?"

So Charles' question was answered. Aubrey still did not know about the cabin, and he was the one who was going to have to tell her, but he had already accepted this. He knew this fact, even before he set the cabin ablaze, but now that the moment was here, Charles felt anxiety.

They kept walking, and Charles said, "Well, your mother and I are about to start building us a house."

Indescribable shock hit Aubrey, like an old tree hits the ground when it falls.

"Do what?"

Charles kept walking, making his way through town to get to his wagon.

"What about the cabin? Where are you going to build?"

"The cabin is gone, but our new house will sit in its place."

"What do you mean the cabin is gone?"

Aubrey was getting angry, especially since Charles kept walking instead of stopping to explain things to her.

"It burned down last night. I burned it down."

"What!" Aubrey shouted, stopping her consistent stride.

Charles however, kept walking. Aubrey's blood was boiling, and though she had always been taught not to disrespect her papa, he was making it very hard for Aubrey to hold her tongue.

Seeing that he wasn't going to stop until he reached his wagon, Aubrey stomped furiously through the thick snow, until she came to the wagon herself. She didn't understand why he kept walking instead of taking the time to look her in the eye and let her know what happened, but there wasn't much she could do about it except for follow him and make sure he saw the fury in her face.

"Why on earth would you burn down our cabin! Explain!" she demanded in a very harsh tone.

Finally Charles stopped what he was doing, standing on one side of the wagon while Aubrey stood on the other side, glaring at him with red in her eyes. He knew she was infuriated.

"Your mother and I need a change. She made it clear that she could not live in the cabin ever again as long as Marty's blood was stained on the floor. We're tired Aubrey, tired of staying in that hotel room."

Aubrey could understand now why the cabin was burned to the ground, but now she wanted to know why she wasn't told.

"Why didn't you tell me what you were going to do? It was my cabin too! Why did you leave me in the dark?"

She shouted at Charles, being unable to remain calm, not caring who might hear.

"You seemed to be busy, and besides, it is none of your concern." Now there was silence between them as Aubrey stared at Charles with her mouth open. How could he say such a thing to her? None of her concern! Charles sighed after he climbed onto the wagon.

"All of your things are at the hotel. I moved them out before. Look, everything is going to be alright."

"I can't believe you!"

Aubrey knew she shouldn't speak this way to her papa, but in her eyes he left her no choice. "Everything is not going to be alright. You burned my only hope of life getting back to normal, and you didn't even consult me! And you are just going about your merry business, acting like everything is fine when it's not!"

"Aubrey . . ."

But she stormed off, not giving her papa a chance to say anything more. She covered her face with her hands as she sobbed, barely being able to see where she was going. Charles could understand her anger, but did not chase after her, because he wanted to give her time to cool off.

Aubrey's world was tipping over all this time, but this was the final push that turned her world upside down. Nothing made sense. Her own papa was treating her like some stranger, by telling her that the cabin she grew up in all of her life being burned down was none of her concern.

What's worse was that Charles had basically been Aubrey's only connection, it seemed, to her own mother, and now she was so angry with Charles that she would not be able to talk to him for a while. He hurt her, and did not even seem to care. Aubrey was absolutely losing her mind, but despite all of the anger, pain, confusion, and distress, there was one thing Aubrey could distinctively determine and be sure of, that she had never been so furious with her papa in her whole life like she was now.

Chapter 7

"Heartbreak"

NO MATTER HOW hard Aubrey tried, she could not hide the fury and pain she was feeling as she worked. Dr. Starks could plainly see that something was wrong, though he did not ask her. He had heard about the fire, and figured that was what bothered his nurse. Aubrey attempted to put all of her feelings and emotions aside so she could do her job, but this was nearly impossible. Dr. Starks personally thought that Aubrey came to work too soon after her brother's suicide, and now she lost her home.

"Aubrey, we're not busy today, so why don't you take the rest of the day off. You need some time off anyway."

"But, what if you need me?"

"I can manage. Besides, I know where to find you."

Aubrey hesitated, holding the broom she was just pushing around. She didn't want Dr. Starks, or anyone for that matter, feeling sorry for her. Aubrey wanted to work, but she had to admit that there had not been many patients today. Reluctantly she agreed, and then put the broom back in its designated corner.

Aubrey put on her coat, bid goodbye to Dr. Starks till the morning, and stepped outside to a bright beautiful day. The sun was straight up in the sky, signaling Aubrey that it was around dinner time. However, Aubrey didn't feel like eating. She knew she needed to, and her stomach even rumbled, but Aubrey was now to the point to where she wanted to just starve, and die. Aubrey honestly did not know why she was being allowed to see another day, when her life seemed to be coming apart.

Praying was something Aubrey was always consistent with, but ever since the night Marty killed himself, Aubrey slowly ceased praying, until she finally did not pray at all. She did not understand why God was allowing all of this to happen. It seemed like every time she turned around, something else went wrong.

Since Aubrey decided to go ahead and eat a little something, she headed back to Esther's store to make herself a sandwich, but before she got to the door, Breu walked up and stopped her. He greeted her with a smile, and she tried to return his kind act, but failed miserably. She could tell that he was excited about something.

"Are you on your lunch break?"

"No, I'm off for the day, but I am about to go eat something."

"Great!" he said cheerfully. "I want to take you somewhere."

"Where?" she asked unenthused.

"It's a surprise. I'll pick you up in half an hour so you can eat."

He quickly kissed her, and then took off running back down the street to the jailhouse. Breu hadn't given Aubrey time to decline, but all she was concerned about at the moment, was a sandwich.

Being the owner of a store, Esther had on hand everything she would need. There was bread already sliced, as well as ham. Aubrey slapped together a piece of ham between two slices of bread, and fixed herself a glass of water from the bucket Esther drew earlier that morning. Aubrey ate as fast as she could, almost choking a few times in the process, but was saved by her glass of water.

When she finished eating, Aubrey spoke with Esther for a moment, and then stepped back outside to wait on Breu. Once out, Aubrey saw the most peculiar thing. Something that Aubrey had never seen in Moline before. It was a peddler's wagon riding down the street with all sorts of trinkets and tonic bottles clanking against each other as they hung in the back. The wagon looked old and worn out, even rotten in some places, with very faint traces of paint here and there decorating the sides.

Aubrey had always heard of peddlers, roaming from town to town, selling all that they could, but never before had she seen one in person. A few minutes after watching the peddler drive his wagon and stop to get off and talk to onlookers, Breu arrived in his wagon.

"Ready?" he asked with a heart-melting smile.

Aubrey didn't answer, but barely smiled as she took his hand and got onto the wagon. With a snap of the reins, the horses began walking. Aubrey still didn't know where Breu was taking her, though it probably wouldn't have been hard to figure out had her mind been clear. Breu's wagon passed by the peddler, who still stood there in the street, obviously trying to make a sale, but the peddler noticed Aubrey. He glared at her, then tipped his hat to her grinning, and Aubrey kept her eyes upon him, until long after they were passed him.

Something about that man made Aubrey feel awkward, but she knew she wasn't in her right mind at the moment. Getting back to her previous state of mind, Aubrey rode beside Breu, but was in a complete different place, her home.

Aubrey did not say a word to Breu during the entire ride to the gazebo, and Breu decided not to say anything either, until they reached their destination. Soon the little gazebo was in view, but instead of stopping the wagon and walking, Breu brought the wagon all the way up to the gazebo, then stopped and said,

"Aubrey, I know how much you love this place, because I love it too." Aubrey just stared ahead.

"There is a story to this place, a secret past I found out. I want to share it with you."

He jumped off of the wagon, and went around it to help Aubrey down. Breu wasn't sure where Hannah's cross was exactly, but he figured he could find it. After searching through dead brush and snow, the cross was discovered. When Aubrey saw it, her thoughts were momentarily engaged in something else beside her pain. Breu began telling Aubrey the story behind that small cross standing in the ground, along with why the gazebo was there.

"That's why there was always oil in the lanterns, because Logan comes out here some nights and talks to Hannah."

The story was so sad Aubrey thought, so unfinished, and cut short.

"Aubrey," Breu began again, "I brought you here not only to reveal the history of this place, but also to tell you that, this place is yours." Aubrey gave Breu a quick glance.

"What?"

"I bought this place. Now I can start building our future home. I want to know all of your ideas, plans . . ."

"You bought this place? When?"

"Yesterday."

"Why didn't you tell me you were going to buy this place?"

"I wanted to surprise you."

Aubrey was now very angry. Not because Breu bought the land she so longed to live on one day, but because he kept his transaction a secret. Aubrey was sick and tired of all the secrecy around her, first with the secret of Marty being her brother, the burning down of her home kept secret by her own father, and now Breu's secrecy in buying Mr. Benton's land.

Was she so little thought of that her voice did not matter anymore? Did her loved ones around her decide to do something, then say to themselves, "Oh, no need to tell Aubrey, she'll adapt," as if she had no feelings? The more Aubrey thought on these things, the more furious she became. She had enough of being left in the dark. Aubrey started walking back to the wagon, without uttering a single word.

"Where are you going?" Breu asked, sensing that something was wrong.

"I've got to get back to Esther's. I told her I wouldn't be gone long." Breu ran to catch up with her, and then helped her onto the creaky wagon. As he got on himself, he asked,

"What's wrong Aubrey? Aren't you happy?"

Sighing heavily Aubrey replied, "No, I'm furious."

"Why?" Breu said confused.

"I'm not mad because you bought this land Breu, but because you didn't tell me. I'm mad because my papa burned our house down, and told me that it was none of my concern!"

"You found out then."

"What? Found out! You mean you knew about it?"

"Yes, but . . ."

"Oh great! Everyone in Moline knew about the cabin except for me, the one who has lived there all of her life!"

Aubrey couldn't help but cry now. Breu understood her pain, and didn't mean to upset her, but realized he had just committed the same wrong with which he had been angry at Charles about, and that was not telling Aubrey his plan. Breu didn't even stop to think that Aubrey might be offended by his secrecy.

"I'm sorry Aubrey. I didn't mean to offend you. I only wanted to surprise you. I should have said something first."

Aubrey knew that Breu was being completely sincere when he apologized, but she was so hurt and angry with everything that she couldn't forgive Breu just yet, and this tore through her heart because Breu was so precious to her.

"It doesn't matter Breu. I can't marry you."

Breu thought he had just been stabbed through the heart with a knife when Aubrey said this.

"What? What do you mean?"

"I'm sorry Breu. Please believe that I'm not angry with you, but my life is like tumbleweed right now, being tossed to and fro, not knowing which way the wind will blow it next. I love you deeply Breu, but I just can't marry you. I've got to figure things out."

"Don't you want me with you, helping you?"

"I do, but as my friend. I can't give you the love and affection you deserve right now. I don't want to lose you Breu, but my life doesn't make any sense. You don't need to be in a relationship with someone like that."

"But I want to be."

"Please take me back to town Breu."

He was now at a loss for words. The plan he had sketched in his mind, to share with Aubrey the good news so it might bring some kind of joy back into her life, completely backfired. All Breu could do for the next few moments was stare at her. She didn't look at him, she couldn't, and now was actually shocked by what she just done. Her insides were burning with guilt and regret for the crime she just committed against her love, breaking his heart, but she couldn't go back now. She too was at a loss for words, and though she wanted to take it all back, Aubrey could only sit there, cry, and feel the icy cold air that now surrounded her, because she had just threw away Breu's loving warmth. After realizing that he wouldn't be able to change her mind, Breu grabbed the reins and gave them a snap.

During the whole ride back into town, Breu's brain was working in overdrive, trying to come up with some way to get Aubrey back. Being so hurt and brokenhearted, he could come up with nothing. Breu couldn't believe Aubrey was pushing him away like this. He was willing to deal with time, space, even distance, but for Aubrey to break off their engagement entirely was something Breu did not want to have to handle.

What Breu meant to be a happy merry occasion, turned out to be one of gloom, heartbreak, and destruction. When they rode out to the gazebo, they were an engaged couple in love with a bright future, but now as they entered back into town, they were only friends, confused, with not even a glimpse of the hope of ever getting back together. Breu stopped the wagon in front of Esther's store, but before he would let Aubrey get down, there was something he had to know.

"Is it someone else?"

Aubrey looked into the eyes of the man she truly loved, but just pushed away. It hurt her to see the pain on his countenance, the pain she voluntarily caused.

"There is no one else and there won't ever be," she answered, with every ounce of sincerity that existed in her being.

She gave Breu one last kiss, which hurt both of them exceedingly, because neither knew when or even if they might kiss again. Then Aubrey climbed off of the wagon and walked into Esther's store, leaving Breu in a lonely desolation which he had felt only one time before, when his family was murdered.

Chapter 8

"Jim"

THE REST OF that day didn't hold any promises in the way of feeling better, but both Aubrey and Breu got through it as best they could until the day was no more. By now, everyone was sick of the snow and bluntly said so in their conversations. Spring was the root of the town's anxiousness, but the more impatient they became, the slower spring would arrive.

Aubrey went to work again the next day, which went against Dr. Starks' better judgment, but he wasn't going to say anything about it. He meant for Aubrey to take at least a couple of days off, yet he could see that she was working to stay busy and keep her mind occupied. Though he wore glasses, Dr. Starks wasn't blind, however if Aubrey wanted to work he would not deny her, because sometimes he really needed the help.

One day, just as Aubrey finished wrapping a little girl's sprained ankle Dr. Starks said, "I am going to check on the Andersons. I'll be back soon, but while I'm gone would you be so kind as to restock the medicine cabinet? We're running low as you can see, and we just received a new shipment."

"Of course."

"And remember to place them . . ."

"In alphabetical order," Aubrey interrupted. "I know Doctor," she said with a smile.

Dr. Starks put on his black coat and was out of the door. The little girl had gone too, being carried out by her big brother leaving only Aubrey in the office. She was quite disappointed because she wanted badly to go on a house call. Dr. Starks had never taken her with him before, and each time he mentioned leaving, her hopes were let down since he would always find Aubrey something to do while he was gone. Aubrey carefully brought out the box packed with straw and glass bottles containing different medicines.

"Alphabetical order," she thought.

Aubrey believed Dr. Starks' alphabet quirks to be quite humorous, but when she really thought about it, having things placed in this order probably helped. That is what her employer told her one day, and she found it to be so.

"When I look for a specific medicine, I don't want to have to look at every single bottle in the cabinet. If they are in alphabetical order, then I can find them easier and quicker," he had explained.

Dr. Starks informed Aubrey of this on her first day of working for him. As she worked with the bottles, Aubrey's mind was taken back to a few weeks ago when Breu was taking her to the gazebo, and she saw her first peddler.

The bottles were what reminded her of it, because the peddler had several bottles of tonics himself in his wagon. Come to think of it, Aubrey had not seen the peddler since that day and she wondered what happened to him.

Then she thought, "He's probably going from town to town as they all do, trying to sell his knick-knacks and what-knots."

Quite frankly Aubrey was glad that he left, because there was just something about him that gave Aubrey the creeps. When he smiled at her that day it didn't seem like a smile of greeting, but of something else which Aubrey couldn't explain. Though Aubrey wasn't a rude person, she honestly did hope she wouldn't have to see that man again.

All of a sudden while Aubrey was in deep thought, the office door swung open abruptly and a man jumped inside. The unexpected noise and man scared Aubrey so much that she dropped one of the bottles she was holding, breaking the glass into several pieces with medicine being spilled all over the floor.

"Jim?" Aubrey asked after realizing that the intruder was no threat. She quickly found a towel to clean up the mess. Jim had no idea that Aubrey was currently employed with his father and obviously did not mean to startle her. Jim joined her on the floor, carefully picking up pieces of shattered glass.

"I'm so sorry Aubrey. I didn't mean to scare you. Are you alright?"

"Yes I'm fine. I just hate that I dropped this bottle. I don't mean to sound rude, but what are you doing here?"

"Oh, I took a few weeks off so I could visit my father. My plan was to surprise him but instead I surprised you."

Aubrey had noticed, from the very first time she met Jim Starks, that he always spoke in seriousness. He hardly ever smiled, yet Aubrey could not tell if this was because he was a miserable human being, or if he simply lacked a sense of humor. Although Aubrey understood why he would never smile at her, because she did turn Jim down when he invited her to the city. Howbeit, Jim never smiled at Aubrey before his rejected proposal, so she came to the conclusion that Jim just didn't like to smile.

"Dr. Starks is out on a house call, but he'll be back soon."

Jim couldn't take his eyes off of Aubrey. She did let him down before, but he believed Aubrey to be the loveliest girl he had ever seen. The mess was cleaned up, and Aubrey thanked Jim for assisting her.

"My pleasure," he replied, then Aubrey gave him a courteous smile and got back to restocking medicine. Aubrey was beginning to feel awkward in Jim's presence. Silence lingered in the room, and it was driving Aubrey crazy. Though she didn't want to, Aubrey tried to begin a conversation with Jim since she figured he wasn't going to.

"So how are things in the city?" she asked, never taking her eyes off of her task.

"Well. Always sick people to tend to in a hospital," he replied as he stood there watching her.

Jim could see her attempt to be civil by starting a conversation, and he tried to return her act of kindness by continuing.

"How long have you been employed here?"

"Since my brother . . ." Aubrey caught herself, and carefully rephrased her statement. "I've been working here for a little while."

Jim wondered why she stopped mid sentence, but he did not pry.

"Are you enjoying it?" he asked.

"Very much. It's keeping me busy, plus this is what I've always wanted to do." She turned to look at him. "Now that I'm able to be a nurse in my own hometown, I think all of my dreams are coming true," but as she said this last sentence, Aubrey knew in her heart that instead of her dreams coming true, they were really falling apart.

If Jim had been raised in a small country town like Moline, then maybe he wouldn't mind opening his own practice and living in one, but he wasn't. Jim loved the city and had no intentions of leaving it, except to visit Dr. Starks. If Dr. Starks' residence were in any other place besides Moline, then Jim's presence would never be seen there, but now Aubrey was here.

He couldn't explain why or how, but when he was around Aubrey it was as if he was captured in a trance. Yes she turned him down once before, but being near her now made Jim want to try again. Jim decided that he needed to leave the office for a while so he could get out from under Aubrey's spell and gather his thoughts. Jim didn't want to leave, but he couldn't just keep standing there staring at her. However, before he left he wanted to know something.

"How is Sheriff Breu?"

Aubrey thought that this question was peculiar, but she replied with, "Fine I guess. I don't see him much."

This puzzled Jim, but he liked where it was going.

"Really? I figured you two would be married by now."

"Funny how things don't work out," she said wishing he would get off of this subject.

"I think I'll head over to the hotel restaurant and get something to eat. Would you like to join me?"

Jim figured that Aubrey would decline his invitation, due to her being the only person in the office who could tend to patients, but he did not want to be impolite.

"Thank you Jim, but I'm sure I would be fired if Dr. Starks came back to see no one restocking his tonics," she said with a polite smile.

"I don't know," Jim replied as he put his coat back on, "you may be more valuable than you think."

After he said this, Jim walked out of the door. Aubrey thought his statement was strange, but she continued her task because she wanted to be finished by the time Dr. Starks returned. She was glad Jim stepped out. He was a good man, and Aubrey wanted to have a friendly relationship with him, but this was rather difficult.

Jim was so quiet and reserved, not allowing anyone inside his thoughts and feelings, which in a way drove Aubrey crazy because she did not know if he held any sort of animosity toward her. Of course he acted as though he didn't, but Jim kept his emotions trapped tightly shut, so how could she ever know?

Breu sat at his desk in deep concentration, beating his fingers on the chair in a slow consistent rhythm. He had been doing this for a while without even knowing it, and Deputy Kevin watched him. Breu had been silent of everything that happened between he and Aubrey, not even telling Kevin who was the one person in town he could trust. Kevin couldn't figure out what was going on, so finally he had to ask.

"What's wrong Breu?"

Breu stopped beating his fingers on the chair and looked over at Kevin who sat across the room.

"Huh? What do you mean?" he asked back.

"C'mon Breu, you've been sitting there for the past hour not saying a word, not doing anything but tapping on your chair. You've told on yourself, so what's wrong?"

He sat there thinking, then took in a long deep breath.

"Aubrey and I are no longer engaged."

This was very hard for Breu to say.

"What?" Kevin asked shocked. "Why?"

"I'm still trying to figure that out. She just broke it off, and it's killing me."

Kevin felt pain for his friend. He knew that the Whittons were going through tough times, and would be for a while, but for Aubrey to leave Breu at the time when she needed him most of all was confusing to Kevin as well.

"I'm sorry Breu. Let me know if there is anything I can do."

"Thanks, but I think the best thing for me to do right now is go outside. This office is depressing."

Kevin smiled, then Breu put on his hat and coat and left the jailhouse. As he walked along the street greeting people and tipping his hat, Breu noticed the visitor in town, who was sitting beside the window in the hotel restaurant eating. His stomach turned at the idea of Aubrey leaving him for Jim, but he knew he couldn't jump to conclusions. Jim had never offended Breu in any way, but still, the timing of Aubrey's decision to break off their engagement, and Jim's arrival seemed too close to Breu.

"All I'm saying is that you should show her you're truly sorry," Tonya pleaded with Ethan as they walked through the snow-covered forest. "If you don't, she'll think of you as some sort of animal, and I know you ain't."

"I don't care what she thinks," he gruffly replied.

"But I do. There is no sense in making an enemy when you could very easily have a friend. Do it for me."

"Alright," Ethan finally agreed giving in. "I'll think of something."

Tonya smiled gratefully at her love and grabbed his hand to hold. They strolled along through the woods, because that was really the only place they could show their love without being caught. Their meetings would not take place everyday, but only when each could sneak away from their chores.

Before chancing an escape however, one or the other would sneakily walk over to the tree that had been the cause of so much controversy between the Woods and Bennetts, to place a note in a deep hole that existed in the midst of the tree. Each day at different times, both Ethan and Tonya came to that particular tree, either to place a note there, or to check for one, and this was how they knew when and where to meet. Laura and Rose thought that their children were acting peculiar when both noticed they would go to that tree everyday, but without suspecting anything, both mothers just assumed their child enjoyed seeing the tree up close.

"How long will we have to sneak around?" Tonya asked Ethan as she became melancholy due to their present situation.

"As soon as I get the job at the bank. Mr. Foley is about to retire, then they will hire me as the new accountant."

Despite Ethan's muscular build and height, he longed to work with numbers. He was a very intelligent individual when it came to mathematics, or life in general, which a complete stranger and some people in town would never guess. Ethan planned on informing his family, and Tonya's, of their commitment to each other once he began working and could begin building a house. Until then, he and Tonya would have to keep their relationship a secret. There was no way he was going to let his mother ruin his future plans, and he knew that she would certainly try.

Ethan wasn't an animal, and he quietly felt wretched about the way he treated Aubrey Whitton. Ethan normally would not have acted so, but when he saw Aubrey looking at them that day, anger and fear came over him. Anger, because he did not want anyone snooping around in their business, and fear because if their relationship was found out prematurely, then all of his plans for the future with Tonya as his wife could be destroyed.

Laura hated Rose so much that if she found out, she would probably send Tonya away. Ethan couldn't let that happen. Ethan knew he should have handled his concerns about Aubrey better, but it was too late now. The past could not be undone, however the future could make up for it.

"Shh!" Ethan commanded stopping Tonya.

Someone was calling for Tonya. It was a man's voice, but it was so far away that the sound was faint. Tonya gave Ethan a look of disappointment when she heard her name being called, because their time together had been cut short.

"Go around so they won't see you coming out of the woods," he instructed her.

"Alright. I love you Ethan."

"I love you too."

They shared a passionate kiss of longing, not wanting it to end. Tonya pulled away and made her way through the trees to her home. Ethan stood there watching her leave, reluctant to let her go. He didn't understand why the two of them had to fall in love when their families were rivals, but Ethan had always loved a challenge, and this he knew, would be the biggest challenge he would probably ever face.

Tonya was worth it to him, and he wasn't going to let a family rivalry destroy what they shared. He was determined, stubborn, and if he stayed in the woods too much longer, would be found out.

Dr. Starks returned to his office at about the same time Jim finished his meal. The house call took longer than Aubrey expected, but she finished restocking the medicine cabinet, still having time to tend to a few patients and sweep the floor. Shortly after Dr. Starks' arrival, Jim returned to the office as well, but Aubrey didn't feel nearly as uncomfortable as she had before, because Dr. Starks was there engaging his son in conversation so Aubrey wouldn't have to.

Aubrey tried to keep herself busy while the two men talked, but she was completely unaware of Jim's focus being on her. His senses were bonded with the conversation at hand, yet his attention remained solely on Aubrey. Jim was quite glad his father hired her, and he pondered on what the future held. Aubrey had already made it clear that she was a country girl incapable and unwilling to leave her country home, and he was ardently in love with the city, not being able to picture himself living in a small place like this.

However, Jim could not get Aubrey out of his mind. When he left this last time to go back home, Jim got so caught up in his work that he hardly had time to think of her. Now that he returned, finding Aubrey closer to him than she was before in working for his father, Jim was being haunted by all of the emotions he had tried to dispose of in the city.

Feelings of curiosity in wanting to know more about Aubrey Whitton, and fondness that he never felt about any young lady he met before. Jim couldn't explain it, but there was something about Aubrey that unlocked new and inexperienced emotions within himself, which no other person was able to bring forth before.

Jim was all but absolutely entranced by Aubrey, from the way her soft smooth voice spoke a word just above a whisper, to the way her skirt swished and elegantly flowed around the room when she moved. He tried to remain focused on the discussion between he and his father, believing the whole time that he was hiding his thoughts and feelings well.

Aubrey was still unsure as to whether or not Jim held a grudge because of her declining his invitation of joining him in the city. If she could see Jim's heart, she would come to recognize that Jim was obviously hurt because of her rejection, but holding a grudge against her was far from the truth.

She worked the rest of the day as though Jim's presence had not upset her routine, listening to the many conversations the father and son shared, but as she listened, Aubrey couldn't stop thinking about her own papa and how he had unnecessarily hurt her. Dwelling on this made her eyes fill with tears, but she dared not let them fall.

If one did escape, she quickly wiped it away before Jim or Dr. Starks noticed. At one point in the afternoon, Aubrey came to realize that she was holding on to the hope of her job healing her pain and solving her problems, but every passing day only dwindled that hope. She needed to go to the One Person she had not spoken to in a while, the Heavenly Father, because only He could heal her broken heart. This healing would not happen overnight of course, but persistently, as long as she relied on Him through faith.

Before Aubrey left for the day, she bid both men goodbye and put on her coat. She intended on going straight to Esther's. Aubrey longed to check on her mother, but she was still so angry with Charles that she decided not to go to the hotel for the risk of seeing him too. She hated feeling this way about her papa, but in her eyes, she had every right to.

As Aubrey walked out of the door, Jim sat there thinking about Aubrey no longer being in a relationship with Breu. If there was no relationship between them, and no other man had claimed Aubrey as his own, then Jim thought every young man in town to be mad.

Chapter 9

"Pleading"

TONYA WOODS AND Ethan Bennett both returned safely home, without anyone even suspecting what they were up to. They longed so terribly to be with one another, but couldn't because they were doing the very same thing Aubrey was, holding fear captive.

Jim planned on staying in Moline for a couple of weeks so he could spend time with Dr. Starks, and though Aubrey was quite happy for both of them, she was beginning to think that the doctor's office wasn't big enough for three. Aubrey was finding it hard to come up with something to do, after all, the floor could only be swept so much in one day.

Dr. Starks still left for house calls, but he never invited Aubrey to accompany him. She couldn't understand this, and came close to politely confronting Dr. Starks about it, but always changed her mind.

Aubrey had not been back to the hotel in a few days, and it was killing her. She was letting her pain and anger control her. Charles knew his daughter was furious with him, but he had a new house to build and his family to piece back together, though the latter he was leaving in God's hands. He believed Aubrey would forgive him in time, but until then, Charles' main priority was in getting his grieving wife back home and out of that hotel room.

Sunday morning rolled around again, with it being the first time Aubrey saw her family in a little less than a week. She didn't speak a word, nor did they. Just seeing her father sitting there in the service, acting like everything was fine, made Aubrey even angrier with him. She didn't hear hardly a word of the sermon, due to her mind dwelling on the past and his heartbreaking words, "none of your concern."

Aubrey was becoming cold and unhappy, with the knowledge pushed into the back of her mind and heart that if she would only place her cares upon the Lord, then her pain could slowly disintegrate. She hadn't fellowshipped with God in a while now, and it was beginning to take its toll. Aubrey was too busy being angry and feeling sorry for herself that she couldn't come to God. Forgiving Charles for what he did was not an option to Aubrey right now, therefore she knew that coming to the Heavenly Father was no option either.

God would not forgive Aubrey until she forgave her papa, her brother, and herself, but this was something she refused to do. In her furious rebellion, Aubrey left the church when services were over, without even giving her parents a goodbye glance.

Sunday turned into Monday, and since it was dinner time now, Aubrey made her way back to Esther's so she could satisfy her grumbling stomach. Being in her own little pain stricken world, Aubrey was startled when someone touched her arm to stop her trot.

"Aubrey," Breu softly said.

"Oh Breu, you scared me," Aubrey replied as she put her hand on her heart.

She stopped walking, and now looked into Breu's handsome face, trying not to go weak in the knees. Aubrey didn't notice until after her heart stopped pounding, that she actually had a smile on her face in Breu's presence.

"I'm sorry, I didn't mean to. I'm not busy at the moment, and I was wondering if you would take a little stroll with me?"

Aubrey was so hungry, and she had a feeling of what Breu was going to say, but no matter how hard she tried Aubrey just couldn't say no to him.

"Yes I'll go."

Breu grabbed her hand, holding it tight, and began walking. Aubrey didn't resist his action. She missed it. The streets weren't that busy, so Breu felt free to hold a personal discussion with Aubrey, without having the fear of someone eves dropping.

"Aubrey, I'm going to be blunt, because frankly I don't know any other way to be. I hate beating around the bush, so I need to know the real reason why you broke our engagement?"

Aubrey knew this conversation was coming, but she wished it hadn't.

"Breu, I wasn't lying when I told you that my life isn't making any sense right now. So much has happened, and I feel so helpless. I am as confused as a lost goose, and I don't think you should be with someone like that. You deserve better."

Breu knew there was more, that this wasn't the real reason, though he believed it may be true about this being the way she really feels.

"Don't you think I need to make that decision? I am a big boy after all, and I don't see you staying in this state of confusion for the rest of your life. Surely you didn't break our engagement for that reason only."

Breu was trying to be understanding, because she was in pain no doubt.

"My family is falling apart. It has already fallen, and I really need to be there for them. I can't do that if I'm married."

Now she was just making excuses, because if anything she was angry with her parents. Aubrey was becoming desperate for reasons why she broke Breu's heart, because she knew deep down that there was no good reason.

"Well, I don't mean to burst your bubble, but Charles and Clara seem to be doing just fine. They are both looking forward to their new house. Don't take this the wrong way Aubrey, but you are doing worse than they are."

"I have good reason to," she replied.

"What do you mean?"

"Look Breu," Aubrey said now being irritated, "my parents may look like they are doing fine, but they're not. When I'm around them, they don't speak, they don't smile, they don't do anything but sit there in grief. It's all over their faces. I have good reason to be worse than they are."

"Why?"

"Because . . ." Aubrey stopped for a moment, but then decided to go ahead and tell Breu what she believed to be going on. "I think they blame me for Marty's death. I blame myself."

Finally the truth came out, and Breu unlocked the hurting secret of Aubrey's heart. He moved close to her as they stopped walking, took her arms and softly said,

"Aubrey, that is absolutely crazy! There is no reason why you should blame yourself."

"Breu, if I hadn't been on that train to begin with, then none of this would have happened. I'd have my brother back, my family back, my home back, and my life back! It is my fault. None of this would have happened if I hadn't come home. Your life certainly wouldn't have been put in danger twice."

She was crying now, being unable to control her emotions. Breu could see how badly she was hurting, and like she felt, he was helpless. All he could do was take her in his arms, hold her tightly, pray, and be there for her, but now he had to convince her to let him be there for her.

"Your brother chose his path in life. You can't lose something you never had to begin with. Don't take this the wrong way, but your family lost your brother not because of you, but because of him. He chose to leave a long time ago and never return except to steal from them. Aubrey, I can tell you without having to think about it, that your parents do not blame you for what happened. You need to go talk to them."

"I can't."

"Why not?"

"I'm angry with my papa Breu. You just don't understand everything that is going on."

"I'm trying to but you keep pushing me away. I love you Aubrey, and I can help you through this if you'd let me."

Aubrey shook her head from side to side, looked up into Breu's face through her tears and said, "I love you too Breu, but I don't deserve you." With that, she broke loose from Breu's strong grip and ran back to Esther's store. Breu stood there in silence, realizing that Aubrey pushed him away because she believed that she was guilty of Marty's death.

Breu stood there thinking of how he was going to make her see that she wasn't to blame, but then he realized, "No, I don't have the power to do that. Only God has the ability to change her mind set and the way she feels."

All Breu could do was pray, and be there for his love. Though not being able to do more made him feel helpless at times, to try to do more might hurt the situation further, and damage their already fragile relationship.

He wanted to go after her, making himself stay with all his might because he knew that she needed time. Only God and time would heal Aubrey now, because nothing else could. Breu slowly turned and walked back to the jailhouse. At least his mind could be put at ease somewhat, since he now knew why his beloved pushed him away. It was obvious to Breu that Aubrey was punishing herself for Marty's death, because she blamed herself.

Aubrey longed to have stayed in Breu's arms. She even shocked herself by leaving him like that, but Aubrey kept saying in her mind, "You don't deserve him."

Aubrey didn't care too much for drama, but she couldn't make heads or tails of her life right now, so she convinced herself that she especially didn't need to be married and confused.

She still couldn't bring herself to do the two things that could begin to piece her life back together again, which was forgive Charles, and let go of the guilt she held onto. Aubrey was living in fear, holding it captive. How simple it would be for her to go to the Father with her burdens, but instead chose rebellion and missed blessings. Aubrey wanted to be in control, but as each day went on the more heartache and pain she felt, which was only a result of her believing that she could be in control of any aspect of her life.

There was only a short amount of time for Aubrey to eat and get back to the doctor's office, but after the talk with Breu, Aubrey lost her appetite. When she finished eating, only because she had to, Aubrey tried to perk up but failed miserably, so she walked back to the doctor's office.

So many times along that walk she caught herself staring down the street at the sheriff's office, hoping that she could see Breu, but he was nowhere to be found. Aubrey wanted to run to him and apologize for everything, restoring their broken relationship.

This is what her heart wanted to do, but her mind said, "He wouldn't take you back now because of the way you've treated him."

Arriving back at Doctor Starks' office, Aubrey opened the door to find the Doctor waiting for her and Jim gone to get something to eat.

"Ah Aubrey, I'm glad you are back. I've got to go to the Sheppard's farm and check on Mr. Sheppard. I'd better take along more medicine just in case he still has that cough," he said as he fumbled around in his pockets and then his black leather bag. "Jim will be back soon, so tell him that I won't be gone long. Can you handle things here?"

Aubrey thought this to be a silly question considering he left her alone to "handle things" all the time.

"Yes sir," she said in a disappointed tone, but Dr. Starks was in such a hurry that he didn't notice.

Apparently Dr. Starks intended on leaving earlier, but while Aubrey was out for dinner, patients came pouring in. Then, just when Aubrey was beginning to suffer from boredom five minutes after Dr. Starks left, the door opened harshly making Aubrey jump, and a young man came in. He was in pain, trying not to show it, but he staggered into the office and went straight to the table. Aubrey wasn't familiar with this strong looking man, though she had seen him around town several times.

"There's something wrong with my shoulder," he informed Aubrey through winces and groans.

Aubrey ran over to him, placed her hands on the shoulder to inspect it and said, "You've dislocated it. What happened?"

She grabbed a pair of scissors to cut his shirt off of the injured area.

"I was working in the barn on a ladder and I lost my balance. When I fell my shoulder was in bad pain."

Aubrey worked profusely, preferring either the doctor or Jim to be here to put his shoulder back in place, but she was all he had, and he was in terrible pain so she couldn't wait. She knew how to handle this situation, but with this man's build, her only concern was having the strength to accomplish it, but all she could do was try.

"He shouldn't be in any more pain than he is right now," she thought. "Alright, bear with me. This is going to hurt."

The young man grabbed the edge of the table so he could squeeze it when he felt horrible pain. Being very careful but efficient, Aubrey used her weight and quickly put his shoulder back in place. The man shouted in pain, but once it was over felt great relief as did Aubrey. She was quite surprised as well at how quickly his shoulder went into place.

They both let out a heavy sigh, but the young man was still sore and hurting. Aubrey went over to the medicine cabinet to get the man some pain medication. When she found the right tonic, she poured the proper dosage into a spoon and gave it to the man to drink. Under any other circumstances, the man would not have taken the medicine, but he was ready for it by now.

"Now this is for the pain. This one dose should do it, but you need to rest your shoulder at least for the remainder of the day. You don't want to irritate it further, or I'll have to be giving you the entire bottle."

"Thank you Aubrey."

This stunned Aubrey that he knew her name, but it wasn't the first time someone knew her and she did not know them.

"I'm sorry about your shirt," she said.

"It's no problem. I'll get the wife to fix it."

She helped him off of the table and walked with him to the door.

"Now remember," Aubrey reminded, "rest the remainder of the day." She figured he wouldn't, because what hard working man would let a sore shoulder keep him from his chores? If he did disobey her order, then he would be the one to suffer for it. Aubrey had warned him, so now it was out of her hands.

The young man only smiled and walked out of the door. He was passed by Jim who was coming back into the office. Jim seemed satisfied by his meal, but was now curious about the man he just passed. Before he could ask anything, Aubrey spoke first.

"Dr. Starks is on a house call, but he said he wouldn't be long."

She placed the pain medicine back into the cabinet.

"Oh. What just happened?"

"That man's shoulder was dislocated, but thankfully I set it back in place."

Jim's eyes widened and he walked back over to the door to open it and take another look at the man.

"You put his shoulder back in place?" he asked in an unbelievable tone.

"Yes, why?"

"I just find it hard to believe that a woman of your size would be able to accomplish such a feat on a man of his build."

Aubrey was beginning to feel a little insulted.

"Well, believe it or not, I did."

She got busy doing little things in the office, letting her last statement be the end of the subject. Aubrey couldn't figure out why Jim acted so shocked by what she did. It was as if he thought her to be some little weakling because of her gender, only being capable of sweeping and making bandages for patients.

She honestly wished he hadn't come back to the office just yet. The more Jim was around Aubrey, the more she surprised him, and the more he became intoxicated with her. He was so smitten at this point that he did not even notice he had offended her.

Aubrey was unsure as to where Jim stood with his perception of women, but Aubrey was in no mood to get in a battle of sexes, if a battle was to be.

Chapter 10

"Building"

WITH CHARLES' GOLDMINE being plentiful, and only his family and Breu being aware of it, he had no problem with the expenses for building his house. As far as anyone else knew, Charles must have saved his money, pinching coins until he became quite wealthy. There was no other way for them to explain how he was able to get what he needed when he wanted on just a farmer's living. No one outside of the family beside Breu knew about the mine, though some did have their suspicions.

Charles wasn't the only one beginning to build. A few days had past and Breu paid for Mr. Benton's land. He was anxious to start building, and while there wasn't a lot of crime right now, Breu wanted to get things going. He didn't say anything to Aubrey about what he was doing because he wanted to give her time. Breu wasn't giving up though, but still had it set in his mind that Aubrey would be his wife.

Breu prayed for Aubrey and his dear friends Charles and Clara everyday. He was strong in his faith, knowing that somehow in someway God would pull this family through their tragedy and hardships. Even if it took decades, Breu was going to keep praying everyday, never giving up on his true love.

Mr. Benton was proud for Breu to own his land. In fact, Breu now made it a point to stop by the old cabin to visit Logan everytime he went out there. Logan enjoyed the visits, and especially liked getting to know Sheriff Breu Lawrence better. Mr. Benton had learned from Breu's visits that he was a strong humble young man, with backbone, and a love for justice.

Breu even noticed that when he came around the cabin, Logan would immediately begin smiling. Logan had been alone for too long, and the frequent visits with Breu were just what he needed.

During one visit Mr. Benton asked, "So when will I get to meet your fiancé?"

The question took Breu off guard, because he no longer had a fiancé, but how could he tell Mr. Benton that? Scrambling for something to say, Breu came up with, "Soon I hope." The story was too long to tell Mr. Benton, but Breu suddenly had an idea. "Maybe she does need to meet him, so she can see that she isn't the only one who has ever felt this kind of pain. I'm sure Logan probably did blame himself for his wife's death, just as Aubrey is blaming herself for her brother's."

"To tell you the truth Logan, I don't have a fiancé anymore," Breu finally decided to admit.

Logan was surprised by what his new friend the sheriff said and asked, "What happened?"

"I don't want to bother you with my affairs."

"Breu, you know how many years I've lived alone. I could stand a little drama in my life." Breu chuckled. "Go ahead son. Tell me what's on your mind."

Breu took in a deep breath and then sighed heavily. He began by telling Logan about Aubrey's kidnapping on the train. He told of how he rescued her, and ended up falling in love with, at the time, this hungry, frozen, and frightened young girl. Breu described how he was friends with Aubrey's mother and father before he ever met her, and finally Breu explained to Logan the events of Marty's unexpected death.

Logan sat there absorbing Breu's story, being able to relate to the pain. Eventually Breu ended his tale, after telling Logan about Aubrey breaking off their engagement because she feels she doesn't deserve him.

"So Aubrey is blaming herself," Logan repeated as he looked at Breu.

"Yes. I pray everyday that God will open her eyes so she can see that it's not her fault."

"Keep praying," Logan said.

"I will, but I would like her to meet you. Maybe if she can talk to you, then your experience with losing your wife will help her."

"We can give it a try," Logan agreed. "But be patient with her. Trust me, this is hard."

Breu left Logan's place that day encouraged and hopeful that the future still held promise for he and Aubrey's relationship. He decided that it would be unwise to rush things, so when Breu felt like the time was right, then it would be that he let Aubrey and Logan meet. Until then, Breu was going to begin building his house. Charles walked into the supply store one morning to find Breu already inside, purchasing quite a bit of supplies.

Curiosity got the best of Charles, so he went over to Breu and said, "Hello Breu. How are you?"

"I'm fine Charles. How are you?"

"Oh I'm making it," he said with a smile as he slapped Breu on the back.

"Jailhouse need repairing?" Charles asked, trying to find out what Breu was up to.

"No, but it's because of the jailhouse as to why I'm buying these supplies. I'm building a house."

"Great!" Charles said enthusiastically. "Aubrey should like that."

"She would have liked that."

"What do you mean?"

"She broke our engagement."

Charles couldn't believe what he just heard.

"Why?" Charles asked.

Breu didn't want to tell Charles the reason because he felt like that was Aubrey's job, however he couldn't keep from it now.

"From what I understand, she blames herself for Marty's death, and she is punishing herself. She told me she didn't deserve me. I argued of course, but it obviously did no good."

"That girl," Charles stated shaking his head with a frown.

"There's more," Breu continued.

Charles couldn't imagine what.

"She thinks you and Clara blame her as well."

Charles let out a deep breath as he thought.

"I see."

Things were at least making a little sense to Charles now.

"I'm guessing she hasn't told you that."

"She hasn't spoken to me in days. I'm sure she's still upset about the cabin."

Breu thought, "Wouldn't you be," but he did not let those words exit his lips.

"Well, if you need any help, just let me know."

"You too, and don't worry about Aubrey. She'll come around. I'll talk to her," Charles informed.

As much as Breu liked the sound of that, he wasn't sure if it would do much good, but he tried his hardest to remain optimistic. After shaking hands the two men bid goodbye, then got back to tending to the business of building their homes.

Clara spent her days in stores buying new fabrics and material to make curtains, quilts, and other things for her new home. She wanted her new house to be more furnished with things that had been lacking in the cabin. Her days were full now with shopping and sewing, passing by quickly more and more, and excitement was slowly beginning to replace some of her pain.

When Charles came back to the hotel from working at their place, he would catch Clara smiling a lot, especially when talking of her plans for their home to be. Seeing her begin to heal helped his healing process as well. They began praying more together and reading God's word together, relying on His strength and power to make it through, and day by day their heartache was slowly taken away. They were beginning to feel peace in its stead, which was God working in their lives as they could easily see.

Aubrey on the other hand couldn't let go of the pain, guilt, and fear. She held them captive, getting spiritually weaker by the day. One afternoon in particular, Aubrey walked down the street and discovered that the man tying down building material was Breu. Dr. Starks had given her the rest of the day off since Jim was with him, and they had only seen three patients. Wanting to remain friends with Breu, she decided to go ahead and walk over to him, to see what he was up to.

"Hello Breu. What are you doing with all of this wood?"

Breu was surprised that Aubrey noticed him, and even more surprised by her curiosity.

"I'm building a house," he said bluntly.

"You are?"

Now she was the surprised one.

"I bought Mr. Benton's land, so now I'm going to build a house. He is a nice old man. I want you to meet him."

Not even paying attention to Breu's last two sentences she replied with, "Why are you building a house?"

Aubrey was being completely self-absorbed at this point, and Breu knew what she was getting at.

"I'm tired of living in the jailhouse. Isn't it funny how we call it a house? Anyway, I'm ready for my own place to settle down on."

"But Breu, I . . ."

"Don't worry Aubrey, I'm building this house only for myself. I know you have no desire to be with me any longer, but I would still like to live on that beautiful property."

"No desire, is that what you think?" Breu only gave her a blank stare. "I want to be with you Breu, but I just can't."

"That doesn't make any sense!" he said more loudly. "Instead of allowing me to be your husband and help you through this, you're pushing me away, tearing my heart out of my chest."

He finished tying down his supplies with a hard yank and then stepped right in front of Aubrey.

"I want you to meet Logan. Don't make any plans for next Sunday after church."

"Breu . . ."

"You're going with me," he stated very sternly.

Aubrey couldn't believe he had just told her what she was going to do. As soon as Breu finished bossing Aubrey, he walked away and climbed onto his wagon without giving her a chance to argue or protest. She stood there watching him leave, still pondering on what Breu had just said about her no longer wanting to be with him.

That was so far from the truth because she loved him so much, and it was nearly killing her not to feel his touch, or his kiss. Aubrey knew that Breu loved her deeply, and was more than willing to help her through this difficult situation, but every time a glint of hope flashed before her eyes, she told herself, "You don't deserve him."

The idea of Breu being with another made Aubrey sick to her stomach, and she realized standing in the street watching Breu drive away, that she was running a good chance of losing him for good. Tears came to her eyes because she honestly didn't know how she could live her life without him.

"How long am I going to live this way?" she thought. "How long am I going to be miserable?"

Aubrey missed Charles and Clara, Breu, and most importantly, she missed fellowshipping with God. As Aubrey turned to go, she had one last thought, "How did I get here?"

Chapter 11

"The Gift"

ETHAN BENNETT HAD felt wretched with the way he treated Aubrey, though he wouldn't dare show it. The more he looked back on that day, the worse he felt. He had acted like an animal, but he decided that he was about to make it right. He realized that he let the fear of his mother finding out about his relationship with Tonya Woods, cloud his judgment and control his actions.

Ethan was quite skilled not only in mathematics, but also in wood working. When he wasn't taking care of chores, or secretly meeting with Tonya, he spent his time working on a new project. Ethan found a perfect piece of squared cedar wood that his father had lying around in his shed, and he was carving Aubrey's name in it. Already Ethan had carved a beautifully crafted border design of leaves and vines, and he was going to attach this piece to a deep cedar wood box with some hinges to make Aubrey a jewelry box.

He hoped that this gift, along with his apology, would make amends for what he did. Ethan was nearly finished with his project and couldn't wait to show Tonya. If she approved, then he would find a time to take the jewelry box to Aubrey. Many times before however, Ethan's work would be temporarily interrupted, either by his parents or younger siblings looking for him. He always worked on Aubrey's jewelry box in his own room, and would hide it when he left.

No one could see what Ethan was doing, because this would raise questions that would eventually lead to the revealing of his secrecy with Tonya. He could not let this happen. Rose didn't think any young lady around them would ever be good enough for her precious son, and Ethan was tired of the way she acted.

He looked forward to the day when he could begin working in the bank, gradually earning his freedom and the right to marry Tonya. However, for now his main focus was finishing Aubrey's jewelry box, and making an apology to her without being found out. Ethan knew his mother would cease his work if she knew who the jewelry box was going to, because she disdained the Whittons, but who didn't she?

If there were no interruptions today, then Ethan would possibly be able to complete his project before the sun went down. A few minutes after hoping this doubtful idea, Ethan heard his mother calling him. Quickly he put all of the project pieces between his mattress and blankets, then went to where he heard his mother's voice. She was standing in the doorway, letting the heat from the fireplace escape from their cabin as she stared at the tree that caused the gulf between her and the Woods.

"Ethan, is it my imagination, or is there something in the tree?" Ethan began to look as well, and noticed that what his mother saw was a note Tonya must have left.

As soon as she realized what it was, Ethan felt fear grip his body and his heart sank down into his toes.

"I'm going to go see what it is," Rose said as she began to take a step. Ethan caught her arm stopping her. She looked at him curiously.

"I'll go check it out mama. You don't need to be out in the cold."

Trying to sound casual, but being unsure as to whether or not it was working, Ethan continued.

"You stay inside by the heat. You don't need to get sick."

Rose did as Ethan said, thinking the whole time that he was acting peculiar, but she continued to stay in the doorway, intent on keeping her eyes on him.

Ethan made his way through the snow to the tree. He did not fear his mother, but rather feared how she would react if she found the note. He wouldn't care how she acted if he could leave and go to his own place, which is what he was waiting for, but since he still lived in her house he would never hear the end of it. That is what he feared and tried to avoid.

Finally he got to the tree, keeping his back facing his mother who cautiously looked on from the cabin. This was easier in summertime, because he could hide in the leaves and branches, but with winter making everything bare, Ethan acted as though he were looking around not seeing anything, when really he grabbed the note and shoved it in his shirt while covering his actions with his torso.

He walked around the tree glancing up and down, making it seem like he was really looking for what his mother had seen, and after spending a few moments at the tree, he walked back to the cabin.

"I didn't see anything out of the ordinary."

AMAZING GRACE WILLIAMS

He chose his words carefully, because for him the note wasn't out of the ordinary, therefore he did not lie.

"Huh. That's odd. I don't see it anymore."

Rose looked curiously at her son.

"Is it time for glasses ma!" Ethan said jokingly, but really trying to set her mind at ease so he would not be caught.

Ethan pulled off his boots, so as to not track in snow, and went back to his room.

"Maybe so," Rose softly answered after he left.

Something wasn't setting easy with her. She was certain that she had seen something in that tree, and when Ethan came back, it wasn't there anymore. Though her son had never lied to her before, Rose knew that something was going on, and she was going to get to the bottom of it.

Ethan tried not to show any hint of fright, but his heart was nearly about to pound out of his chest. He walked back to his room, shut the wooden door, and sat on his bed. As he sat there, he listened for any sound of footsteps coming near his door. There was silence, but Ethan was not going to take any chances, so he sat there as still as a flower on a grave, hearing nothing but the pounding of his heart.

After a few minutes more, he finally began to calm down when no sound was heard. Ethan took the note from his shirt very gently so he would not make the paper crinkle and make too much noise. Carefully unfolding it, what Ethan expected to read wasn't there.

Instead was written, "I know what you are hiding. I am watching you."

Immediately upon reading this frightening note, Ethan began to feel terror, sickness, and anger.

"Who on earth wrote this letter?" he thought. "Aubrey? No, she wouldn't do something like this. Surely someone in Tonya's family hasn't caught us. What about Sheriff Breu? I made him pretty upset with the way I treated Aubrey. Why would a sheriff do something so sly?"

Ethan's mind was running rampantly, trying to figure out who could have done this, yet still keeping in mind what the note said, "I am watching you." That meant that it was no longer safe to use the tree for communication to Tonya.

"How long has this person been there watching?" Ethan then thought. Anger and rage was rushing through his veins, because he suddenly realized that Tonya might not be safe. He could not take his eyes, or his mind off of the note. The handwriting was scratchy and rough, not at all fashionable and orderly. Ethan didn't recognize the handwriting, but he was going to take it to Tonya somehow, to see if she recognized it. How he was going to get to her though since he could no longer use the tree, was the puzzle Ethan would have to figure out.

If Tonya didn't recognize the handwriting either, then Ethan decided that he would confront Sheriff Breu about it. Until then, Ethan was going to be very cautious when leaving the cabin, but he was so anxious to warn Tonya that he was afraid he would go mad.

"I'll just have to keep my eyes open and on both places," he told himself, being unsure if this was some kind of childish prank done by either his or Tonya's younger siblings, or if there was some kind of madman on the loose.

From now on, Ethan would be looking over his shoulder constantly, being uneasy with who he could trust. He hadn't noticed until now that his hands were trembling, so he softly folded up the piece of paper, placed it in his pants pocket so he could keep it with him at all times, and got out Aubrey's jewelry box.

Now that Ethan was nervous, he needed something to occupy his hands with, so he worked profusely on the jewelry box, intent on finishing it today. He had to get to town as soon as he could, and he wanted to deliver Aubrey her gift while there.

Aubrey was working in the doctor's office, cleaning the wound of a small boy. Apparently the little boy had been playing on one of the horse troughs in the street and fell giving himself a cut on his leg. Aubrey was briefly taken back to her escape through the woods when she injured her own leg.

"Alright, that should do it," she informed the little boy, then she helped him down from the table, and led him out of the door.

Dr. Starks was on yet another house call, but this time Jim stayed in the office with Aubrey, much to her dread. The child was now gone, so Aubrey began putting away the leftover bandaging materials.

"So how do you like working for Dr. Starks?" Jim asked over his book.

"I really enjoy it," Aubrey replied, "but I wish I could go on house calls."

"House calls? Why on earth would you want to do that?"

Aubrey was surprised by his question.

"Why not? I enjoy helping people, so why should I be limited to the office?"

"But you're a nurse," Jim said rather snobbishly.

Aubrey wasn't sure what he was getting at, but she was becoming offended.

"Yes I'm a nurse. So what?"

"Nurses don't belong outside of the office," he stated bluntly.

Aubrey couldn't believe what she just heard! So Jim is male chauvinist. She really was dumbfounded, trying to find something to say.

"What do you mean? A nurse is just as capable of tending to patients as a doctor."

"Well sure, if the nurse is a man."

Aubrey's mouth dropped open.

"So this is the real Jim!" Aubrey thought.

Jim stood to his feet laying his book down and walked over to Aubrey. Before she could argue his point by saying something else, Jim spoke again.

"Aubrey, I know I've already revealed my affections for you, but I am leaving tomorrow afternoon, and I would be so delighted if you would reconsider and join me in the city. We would have a marvelous time, one that I am certain you would not regret."

Again Aubrey was rendered speechless as Jim left her with one last statement.

"Think about it."

She was so shocked by his male chauvinism that she couldn't speak. Now she was angry as she stood there looking at the door Jim just departed through.

"How can he be so pig-headed!" she thought. "Why would he want me to join him in the city, when he obviously thinks of women as just a little more valuable than dogs? I can't believe he thinks nurses, or women rather, belong only in the office. I guess I should be happy that he allows that privilege, instead of thinking women only belong in the kitchen and bedroom!"

Aubrey was absolutely furious.

"Wait," she said aloud this time, "if he thinks that way, then Dr. Starks might as well. Maybe that's why he won't ask me to join him on house calls, because he believes that I belong only in the office."

Now things were making sense to Aubrey. She was beginning to resent Dr. Starks for possibly being the root of Jim's sprouted male chauvinism, but she was going to try her best not to show it. Jim never came back to the office, which disappointed Aubrey, because she wanted to decline his offer yet again, hopefully in a polite manner.

Soon the day was spent, and Aubrey was glad that tomorrow was Sunday, though she did not want to see Charles. For Aubrey, that night was one of those that seemed as if morning arrived as soon as you shut your eyes to go to sleep. Aubrey awoke tired, but she got up and dressed, then left for church with Esther. As was the ritual, Charles and Clara came in just as service was about to begin, not having any time to speak to Aubrey, not that she wanted them to.

Rose and Ingrid had their little gossip session before the service began, and without anyone knowing it, Ethan sneakily got behind Tonya Woods and whispered in her ear, "Meet me after church in the woods."

As Aubrey opened Esther's worn out bible to turn to the passage the pastor quoted, the name "Henry Worthington" popped out at Aubrey again as usual.

She felt as if she knew this man, since she saw his name so much, but really she knew nothing about him at all. And just like other Sundays past, Aubrey left the church as soon as the dismissal prayer ended, not speaking a word to her parents. This made her quite miserable, but she was still angry with Charles. He didn't have to treat her that way.

Aubrey wanted to go back to Esther's place and rest. She felt so tired and sleepy, but her job wasn't stressful. Thinking on her way, Aubrey realized that she could count on one hand how many people she even spoke to anymore. Breu, on occasions, Dr. Starks, Jim, and Esther. This wasn't like her.

Normally she greeted people as she passed them on the street, but Aubrey hadn't felt like doing that in a long while. Deep down Aubrey knew that she couldn't live the rest of her life in this state, miserable, lonely, and full of guilt. Dwelling on these facts made her even more tired and sleepy. Aubrey just wanted to take a nap, and for a little while at least, forget about the way her life was going.

Once she got into Esther's bedroom, she took off her coat and boots and then went limp, collapsing on the bed and a few moments later, falling asleep. Ethan met Tonya in the woods directly after church and showed her the note. He told her about that day, and asked if she thought the handwriting could belong to one of her siblings.

"No," she replied, and Tonya now felt the same fear Ethan had felt upon reading the note, but to a greater degree.

"Watch your back, and be careful. I don't know what's going on, but I'm going to find out."

He told her not to use the tree any longer because it wasn't safe, and after their hurried visit, Ethan found his horse and rode back into town. A couple of hours later, Aubrey awoke, feeling more rested than she had before, but all of the things she wanted to forget returned without delay. Esther wasn't anywhere to be found, so Aubrey decided to take a little stroll through town to get some fresh air. Aubrey had not gone far when Ethan Bennett approached and stood directly in front of her.

"Hello Aubrey."

"Ethan," she replied, being unsure as to what this was about. Ethan took in a deep breath, which pushed his already broad chest outward even more, making him seem even taller than what he actually was.

"I just wanted to apologize to you for acting so brutishly the other day. I'm not like that, and I hope you won't regard me as a heathen. I'm sorry."

Aubrey could see his honesty.

"Thank you Ethan. I accept your apology. What I said that day was the truth. Your relationship with Tonya is none of my business, and your secret is safe with me."

"I know. But whether it is or isn't, I should have never treated you like that. Here, I brought you a gift."

Ethan had kept his hands behind his back until now, and when he brought them forward, Aubrey saw a cedar jewelry box with her name carved in it and a bouquet of pink camellias Ethan had picked from his mother's garden. She was shocked by Ethan's act of kindness, and really didn't know what to say.

"Oh Ethan, you didn't have to do that."

"I know. I wanted to."

She took the gift he held out to her, smelling the camellias and trying not to cry.

"Thank you so much. This really means alot to me."

Ethan smiled, and Aubrey gave him a hug. Finally something in her life worked out. Ethan and Aubrey were now friends, who held a secret with each other that bonded them closely. These two had never been close before, but Aubrey could distinctly see a great maturity in Ethan Bennett of which his mother lacked. Both felt weight lifted off of their shoulders because of their new friendship, and Aubrey saw Ethan as a gentleman for the first time. Ethan knew he could trust Aubrey and intended on helping their friendship grow.

After their friendly embrace, both shared a smile and bid each other goodbye. Aubrey held her gift close, being unable to take her eyes from the beautiful designs and craftwork that Ethan had put into the jewelry box, and that God put into the camellias. She continued walking, however slowly strolling along the street until she came near the jailhouse. Suddenly again, Aubrey was confronted by someone.

"Aubrey," Jim said with his bag in his hand.

Quickly the memory of Jim's invitation, along with his departure being today hit Aubrey.

"Oh, Jim." Aubrey was taken from her peaceful state of mind, to wishing she was somewhere else at the moment. "You are about to leave?"

"Yes, will I be going alone?"

Aubrey hated to do this to him again, but he brought it upon himself she settled in her mind.

"I'm sorry Jim. I just can't go with you. There are alot of things going on in my life right now that I need to stay here and sort out. I don't expect you to understand, but I do thank you for the invitation."

She wasn't going to say this, but Aubrey really couldn't see herself with a male chauvinist. Jim looked at the box and camellias Aubrey carried and assumed that she and Breu were back together. He gave her one last stare, and without returning any sort of reply Jim took his bag and left. Aubrey was sure that this time he was angry with her, but she couldn't help that. Aubrey turned to keep walking down the street, wanting to take her gifts inside.

Breu sat at his desk feeling sick to his stomach as he glared through the window. He had been studying new wanted ads when he looked up and saw Jim talking to Aubrey, with her holding some kind of box and flowers. Breu didn't see Jim give her those items, but Breu assumed that he did. Breu knew that Jim had feelings for Aubrey, so who else could have given her those things?

Aubrey had told Breu before that she still loved him and that there wasn't another, but from what he just seen, Breu was beginning to believe that he had lost her for good. Did she love Jim now? If she wouldn't keep Breu because of the situations in her life, then why would she take Jim? Breu didn't know what was going on, but he was about to confront Aubrey and find out.

His thoughts were briefly interrupted when Ethan Bennett walked through the door. Breu was surprised to see him, considering how their last meeting was one of anger and warning. Ethan approached Breu's desk, and both men stared at each other.

"I apologized to Aubrey, and I owe you an apology as well," Ethan stated, not mentioning the gift he had given her.

"Don't worry about it," Breu replied.

"I was wondering if you have ever seen this before."

Ethan unfolded the strange note he pulled from the tree and laid it on Breu's desk. Breu picked it up and read it.

"That's creepy. No I've never seen it before. Why do you ask?" Ethan didn't want to go into detail with Breu, so he kept it simple.

"I just wondered, that's all."

"Hey, you're not in some sort of trouble are you?" Breu asked very seriously.

"No, it's nothing like that. I just wasn't sure if maybe you recognized the handwriting."

Breu studied the note again.

"Sorry, I can't imagine who would have written that."

Ethan nodded his head, being relieved that Breu wasn't the one behind it, but also feeling disappointed because he still had no idea who was. Breu handed him the note back.

"Alright, thanks."

Ethan folded the note, put it in his shirt, and turned to go.

"If you are in any sort of trouble, you let me know," Breu commanded.

"Thanks again," Ethan stated, then he left the Sheriff's office.

"That was weird," Breu thought, but the words of that note gave Breu an uneasy feeling.

Something was going on, and if it turned out to be some kind of joke, then Breu was going to be upset. Ethan got on his horse and headed for home. Being unaware of his mother's snooping friend watching him earlier, Ingrid saw Ethan ride off. She had a new itch, one that would drive her nearly insane until she could tell her dear friend Rose Bennett that her son Ethan was in love with Aubrey Whitton!

Ingrid couldn't believe her eyes when she covertly observed Ethan giving Aubrey a jewelry box and some pink camellias. Her jaw dropped, but slowly turned into an evil grin upon seeing this. Then she saw them share an embrace!

"They must be an item!" Ingrid thought, and now she was trying to come up with a way to go and tell Rose.

She knew Rose would have a fit if Ethan was seeing Aubrey. Ingrid also knew that Rose was the kind of woman who thought that her son was too good for any girl in Moline, so this was sure to rise up a stink, which is what Ingrid thoroughly enjoyed doing.

Though the Whittons could somehow afford what they needed when they wanted, unlike most folks, the Whittons were still beneath Rose and Ingrid in the two women's minds. Somehow she had to get to Rose, and quick!

AMAZING GRACE WILLIAMS

Chapter 12

"Colonel Bragg"

AUBREY SAT NEAR the fire admiring her new jewelry box. She couldn't get Ethan off of her mind. It was so kind of him to go through so much trouble just to apologize. He was a good person, and Aubrey felt that he deserved Tonya, because she was good-hearted as well. Outside was freezing with the sun down, and Esther sat by the fire also reading a book.

Never before had it dawned on Aubrey to ask, but suddenly she found herself asking Esther, "If you were a slave, how did you learn to read?"

The question didn't bother Esther, but rather brought back painful memories.

"My pappy taught me when I was a small child."

Aubrey knew she shouldn't pry on such a touchy subject, but she had to ask one more question.

"How did he learn?"

Esther looked over her book at Aubrey, making no expression on her face.

"He was well educated."

That was all she said so Aubrey took that, along with her subtle actions, as a hint not to ask anymore questions.

The night went on, bringing an early sleep to some, and a light sleep to others like Ingrid, who couldn't wait til the morning came. Everyone awoke the next morning still a bit sleepy, but ready to face another week. The days went on, and the snow still lay on the ground. Every now and then Charles would call on either Kevin or Breu to help him with building his house, but Charles was taking his time, offering work to any able man who needed a job.

Breu began building his home too, but at a much slower rate since he couldn't find time. That Friday afternoon, Breu had been working out at the gazebo, but had to ride back into town for more supplies. After arriving, Breu spotted someone he thought was dead, someone he thought he would never see again, the one who had caused his pain and suffering from childhood. Colonel Bragg, the man who was behind the massacre that murdered Breu's people.

Colonel Bragg was a very large, rough looking fellow. He stood at around six foot and five inches tall, weighing close to two hundred fifty pounds. His clothes were filthy and worn, but he still wore his cavalry jacket that was now a heavily faded blue. No one was with him, and he got off of his horse with a hard thud. Breu watched as Colonel Bragg entered into Esther's store. Had it not been for someone informing the survivors of the massacre the name of the man who slaughtered their tribe, then Breu would not have known it, however his face Breu never forgot and never would.

Now that Breu had the law backing him, he was going to arrest Colonel Bragg for the murder of innocent people, not for revenge, but because at the time of the massacre there was a peace treaty between this Cherokee tribe and the American government. The cavalry's invasion was completely unexpected, and absolutely unnecessary. It was not suppose to happen, and shouldn't have happened.

Breu's people posed no threat to the government, and cooperated with U.S. forces during any situation. The Cherokees wanted peace, but instead found death. Over time, Breu was able to forgive the men who murdered his people, including Colonel Bragg, but he hadn't forgotten.

He stopped what he was doing, completely intent on arresting the Colonel, forgetting about the building of his house momentarily. Steadily Breu walked to Esther's store, being unafraid, but anxious to finally come face to face with the person who had caused him so much grief as a child. Breu was sure that Colonel Bragg would have no clue as to who Breu was, but he was soon about to find out. His heartbeat accelerated as he went up the steps of the store, but suddenly he came to a stop as he remembered something.

Quietly within himself, Breu said a prayer asking for God's guidance, protection, and wisdom. After finishing his earnest yet hasty prayer, Breu took a deep breath, and then walked inside the store. Colonel Bragg didn't notice Breu come in, but stood at the counter waiting for whoever managed the place, which was Esther. It took all of the courage Breu could muster, plus what God gave him, to stand there and face his nightmare.

As Esther hurriedly went to the other side of the counter she asked, "May I help you?"

Without thinking about it Breu spoke before the Colonel could.

"He won't be needing any help Esther."

Immediately Colonel Bragg turned to see who had the guts to interrupt his purchase and stick his nose in the Colonel's business. He studied Breu through his cold eyes, not showing any reaction through his wrinkled, scarred, hairy countenance. The Colonel noticed the star that shone on Breu's shirt, but had no fear or respect, because in his eyes he was the law.

Esther averted her attention to both men, back and forth, not saying a word, yet knowing that something terrible was about to happen. She inwardly wondered why trouble always seemed to find her store, because it was here that Rose Bennett and Laura Woods had their spat.

"Mind your own business boy, or someone's gonna get hurt," Colonel Bragg said gruffly, showing Breu no respect for his authority.

Anger burned within Breu, but quickly had something to reply.

"Mind my own business like the Cherokee's were doing when you slaughtered them."

Colonel Bragg then completely turned his body to face Breu, and both men stared each other down.

"Bragg, you're under arrest for the murder of innocent men, women, and children of the Cherokee tribe."

Breu did not address him as Colonel Bragg, because a true Colonel would not have committed such a horrific act in Breu's eyes. The Colonel remembered what the sheriff was talking about even after all these years, but he took this as an insult.

"I don't know who you are boy, but the name is Colonel Bragg, and if anybody is the law around here it's me."

Breu tried his best to remain calm, relying on the Heavenly Father to keep his finger off of the trigger, but it was torturously difficult. Just in case there was gun fire exchanged, Breu didn't want Esther to get hurt.

"Esther, get in the back," he commanded, and without any hesitation or question she did what he said.

Once she shut the door, she listened intently with her ear pressed hard against the wooden door, praying inwardly that trouble wouldn't come. Breu broke the deafening silence by rebutting, "A colonel is a servant, not a mass murderer, one expected to carry out orders, uphold his honor and integrity, and protect those under peace treaties. You are anything but a colonel, and God will reward your actions."

Colonel Bragg smirked, but wasn't about to let some young boy get away with insulting him like this, even if he did call himself a sheriff.

"You picked the wrong man to mess with boy. Peace treaty or no peace treaty, Indians don't belong on this land, and I only wish I had killed more."

After this heart wrenching statement, the Colonel speedily pulled out his pistol to kill Breu, but Breu drew his gun just as fast and Esther heard two gunshots which made her scream.

"Oh no!" she cried, afraid to go back into the store, but the thought of Breu being hurt pushed her to go. When she rushed through the door she saw gun smoke and the Colonel lying on his back with a gunshot wound dead center in his chest. She looked up and saw Breu with his gun still drawn, ready to shoot again if need be.

The Colonel was dead, and Breu trembled from his near death experience. Esther ran over to Breu and embraced him, checking him out for any wounds because he had not yet said anything.

Breu put his gun back in place, looked into Esther's worried eyes and said, "I'm alright Esther."

Men began rushing into the store to see what the shots were about, and a great commotion could be heard outside. The men saw the Colonel lying dead on Esther's floor and knew that Breu must have done it, but had a good reason. Without explaining anything, Breu told the men to pick up Bragg, and take him to the undertaker. After this incident, anyone who doubted Breu's skill and capability doubted no more. A new respect and fear entered the people of Moline when word spread about the sheriff killing a United States colonel.

After making his order, Breu left the store to go back to the office because he needed to make a report. Aubrey was one of those who came out into the street to investigate the shooting, but when Breu came close to her, he walked on past Aubrey not saying anything.

"Breu! Breu!" Aubrey shouted, but he didn't turn around.

He didn't want to turn around and explain to Aubrey what happened. Breu believed that Aubrey gave up the right to know what was going on in his life, but he did hate walking away from her. He needed time alone in his office to complete a report while it was still fresh on his mind, but to be honest, Breu was getting tired of being at Aubrey's every beck and call when she chose to no longer be his.

Aubrey was upset that Breu ignored her, but was relieved to see him alright from whatever just happened, with that still being a mystery to her. She decided to leave Breu alone and go find out about the gunshots.

As Breu sat at his desk filling out a report, he thanked God that he was still alive, though he knew where his soul would eternally abide had he died. It bothered Breu that he just took a man's life, even if it was in self-defense, but Breu had faith that God knew his heart. God knew that Breu gave Colonel Bragg a chance to be arrested peacefully, and that Breu didn't kill him for revenge. Had this happened several years earlier, then Breu would have killed the Colonel for revenge, but over time God had calmed and comforted Breu's angry heart. He couldn't believe that the Colonel hadn't already been arrested for his crimes against the natives, but the incident had probably gone unknown to the rest of the country. If anyone did realize that the Cherokee tribe had been killed without cause, then it was common for them to look the other way. However, Breu couldn't look the other way, because he had been there.

Deputy Kevin was in the office when the shots were fired, but as soon as he heard them he raced across town being one of the first men in the store. Now that Breu left, Kevin was presiding over the situation. He was in shock too, because nothing of this severity ever happened in Moline, though he was always ready in case it did. Kevin didn't even know that Breu had returned to town from working out at his new place, so he felt a certain amount of relief to find that Breu was already at the scene and saw what happened. Kevin just hated that Breu had been involved.

After Deputy Kevin finished at Esther's, he walked out into the street among the crowd and shouted, "Everybody get back to what you were doing. It's all over, there's nothing more to see."

Some people were disappointed by Kevin's announcement because they still had no idea what happened, and curiosity burned within them. Esther had no damage to her store, except for a bullet hole in the wall behind where Breu stood. She assumed the bullet missed Breu and landed in the wall, to which she was grateful.

The Colonel was taken to the undertaker, to either await information on where to take his body next, or to await burial. Aubrey went back to work at the doctor' office trying to process what just happened, and the fact that she somehow almost lost Breu. This scared her to no end, and she began contemplating on if he had just been killed. Would she be able to live with herself if he had, knowing that he died with a broken heart which she had caused? Deputy Kevin stomped through the snow back to the jailhouse so he could find out what happened himself.

"What was that all about?" he asked Breu as he came inside the sheriff's office, hanging up his coat and hat.

"That man was under arrest for the murder of a Cherokee tribe several years back."

Breu didn't go into detail, because only he and Aubrey knew his secret, and he couldn't allow the town to find out that he was half Indian, because they might fire him.

"He wasn't willing to go. He drew his gun on me, but I was quicker. It was self-defense."

Kevin sighed shaking his head back and forth, finally understanding what happened, and glad that Breu was alright.

"Next time, let me know you're in town before you go off chasing bandits. I thought it was two civilians out there."

"Sorry," Breu replied, "I only came back to get more supplies. I wasn't intending on arresting anybody, much less killing them. I hate that I killed him."

Breu was being completely sincere when he said this.

"I'm not! Better him than you."

Breu knew Kevin was right, but there were things he wanted to find out from the Colonel, things he planned on asking Bragg once he got him in jail. Breu had always wanted to ask the perpetrator, "Why?" Colonel Bragg at least answered that question before he died. He absolutely hated Indians, and thought of them as scum. Breu just wished that his people, and his parents, didn't have to die because of one man's racist and sadistic opinion.

After finishing the report, Breu raised his shirt because he felt a pain on his side that had intensified as he calmed down from the shooting. He was dripping blood from where the Colonel's bullet grazed his side. There was a nasty slit in his flesh, and as he kept investigating he noticed a hole in his jacket where the bullet went through, the same jacket he had put on Aubrey on those cold nights of her rescue not so long ago.

Breu thought he felt his heart leap, because only divine intervention made that bullet miss its intended target. Especially since Bragg was a skilled shooter being a colonel, and at that short range. He stood to his feet and turned to face Kevin when he got to the door.

"I've got to go see the doc. I'll be back."

If Aubrey still wanted to know what happened, then now was her chance.

Breu made his way through the snow-covered street, and as he walked, he said, "Thank you Lord, for making that bullet miss my gut."

Chapter 13

"Visit"

D R. STARKS HAD been called to go to the undertaker so he could officially pronounce the colonel dead, so when Breu came into the doctor's office, Aubrey was the only physician available.

"Breu," she exclaimed, shocked at his presence. "What happened?" He walked to her, raised his shirt, and told her about his run in with the colonel.

"His bullet grazed my side."

Aubrey could see his wound, and immediately began gathering bandages and medicine.

"So he was the man responsible for . . ." Aubrey didn't want to finish the sentence because she was unsure as to how it might affect Breu.

"Yes."

As she mended Breu's side diligently working, Aubrey asked, "Breu, why didn't you stop in the street?"

Breu took a moment and then answered, "I just killed a man Aubrey. I didn't feel like explaining anything."

Aubrey left the discussion at that, still working on Breu's side. There was an obvious intensity between the two. Not one of anger and hate, but on the contrary, one of longing and desire. Aubrey tried not to show the weakness that touching Breu's abdomen caused, and Breu couldn't help but watch her and long for her touch.

This particular moment together was difficult for the both of them, wanting each other with love's desire, yet having to retrain themselves because their relationship was no more. Aubrey finished, having placed a bandage over the wound. She prepared more so he could take them with him.

"You need to change your bandage daily to keep the wound clean." Aubrey handed the bandages to Breu.

"I'll pick you up after church at Esther's."

Then Aubrey remembered how he was going to be taking her to meet Mr. Benton.

"Alright," she agreed.

Breu fixed his shirt, and then slowly walked to the door.

After he had the door open Aubrey said, "Breu, I'm so glad you're alright."

Breu stood there for a brief moment looking at his love, then he shut the door and walked back over to Aubrey. He grabbed her face gently, and kissed her passionately. Breu didn't care if their relationship was over, or if she now belonged to Jim. God gave him a chance at life, so he was going to go after the desires of his heart.

Aubrey didn't resist, but missed Breu's love so much that she welcomed it. Breu raised his head staring into Aubrey's eyes, then without saying another word, left the doctor's office. Aubrey stood there in a trance, and finally had to sit down because of the effect Breu's kiss had on her. "Maybe there is still hope for us," she thought, though she accepted the fact of it being her fault if there wasn't.

Breu walked down the street and ran into Dr. Starks.

"You alright sheriff?" the doctor asked looking Breu over.

"Yes. A bullet grazed my side but Aubrey fixed me up," he said holding up the bandages she had given him.

"Good good," the doctor replied. "Glad you're okay."

After giving a slap on Breu's shoulder the doctor went back to his office, and Breu went back to his. After Breu made sure that things in town calmed down, and that Kevin had things under control, Breu went about his original business of buying more supplies to work on his house. He grew tired of having to assure each person who confronted him that he was alright. Breu was anxious to get back to the gazebo, because his day was slowly fading away.

Aubrey seemed to be under a spell for the rest of the day, the spell of Breu's passionate kiss. The more she dwelled on that moment, the more she wanted to repair the damage she had caused.

"Could it be that I am allowed happiness? Am I wrong for punishing myself?" These were the questions that flooded her mind, but her heart answered those questions for her with a "yes."

Ingrid had not yet had the chance to speak with her friend Rose Bennett about what she saw Ethan do, but Sunday was in two days, and Ingrid would be sure to tell her then. She had nearly gone mad from having to wait for so long, but she would have her chance, and Ingrid couldn't wait. Ingrid and her husband hardly ever spoke, one reason was because when they did communicate, Ingrid was either bossing him around or griping at him because of something. Another reason why they never spoke was because her husband just liked to be alone, away from the gossip, the griping, and the bossing.

When they first got married, they were very much in love, but over time grew apart. He still loved her, but didn't like the person she had become. Ingrid's husband realized that her behavior began changing when she met and became friends with Rose Bennett, and to be honest, he couldn't stand that woman.

Ethan now spent his days looking over his shoulder. He now lived his life as if someone was constantly watching him, always being alert. Ethan didn't meet Tonya in the woods as often as before, because he did not want to put her in any more danger than she might already be in. The tree held no more notes, however Ethan knew that the situation hadn't disappeared.

Finally Sunday came again, and as soon as Ingrid saw Rose Bennett, she jumped at the chance to tell her what her son had been up to. At first Rose became defensive, insisting that Ethan would not stoop so low as to have feelings for Aubrey Whitton, but as Ingrid kept telling her what she saw Rose thought, "That would explain his peculiar behavior."

"I'll ask him myself," Rose replied, not showing Ingrid any sign of worry or belief.

In her mind though, Rose believed her friend's words.

Aubrey was quite curious and surprised not to see Charles and Clara in the service that morning. Though anger at her father still raged on within Aubrey, she hoped they were alright. She would have no time to check on them, because after church Breu would be taking her to meet Mr. Benton.

After the service, Aubrey had just enough time to get a bite to eat before Breu showed up. He helped her onto his wagon and they left. Neither of them said anything at first, but the silence was too awkward for Aubrey, so she spoke.

"How is your side Breu?"

"It's fine."

That was all he said. This wasn't like Breu. Usually he conversed well but today he didn't have much to say. There was a long silence again, and Aubrey had enough.

"Breu, why are you taking me to meet Mr. Benton? And why won't you talk to me?"

"I'm sorry. I've just got things on my mind."

"Like what?"

"Bragg. I hate that I killed him."

"Breu, you can't blame yourself."

"Funny you should say that. I've been trying to convince you of the same thing. That is why I am taking you to meet Mr. Benton. Not only because you should know him, but also because you need to hear what he has to say."

"Breu . . ."

"When did you begin blaming yourself? Was it when you suspected that your parents did, or as soon as it happened?"

Aubrey brought back the memory of that night, as painful as it was. She took a moment to gather her thoughts.

"When Marty held me in the cabin, I heard mama calling out to him. I heard the love and fear in her voice. I began blaming myself when I realized that mama hadn't seen him in several years, and when he did finally come home, he had to kill himself because I was there in the way of what he wanted. Maybe if I would have just given him the gold then he'd still be alive, and mama wouldn't be so down."

Breu realized that maybe Clara is the one Aubrey really needed to be speaking to. If she saw that her mother didn't blame her for Marty's suicide, then perhaps she would let go of her guilt. Either way, Aubrey still needed to meet Logan, if anything else to get her mind on something besides tragedy.

Aubrey was surprised to see the old worn down shack, but she remembered what Breu had told her about Mr. Benton living alone for many years, so Aubrey figured that this was to be expected. Before she knew it, they were climbing the creaky rotting steps, and then Aubrey saw Mr. Benton come to the door.

"Hello Breu!" Logan said in an excited tone.

Aubrey wasn't expecting a jolly man to greet them at the door, but she was rather glad. Her hope was that Mr. Benton wouldn't be melancholy and awkwardly silent.

"You must be Aubrey," Logan continued as he held out his hand for Aubrey to shake.

"Yes, it's nice to meet you Mr. Benton."

"Please call me Logan."

After the introduction and shaking hands, Logan motioned for the two young people to come inside near the warmth of the fire.

"Actually Logan, I have to run a quick errand," Breu informed not entering the house.

Logan looked surprised, as did Aubrey. Breu hadn't planned this unexpected errand, however after speaking with Aubrey, Breu felt it necessary. Aubrey gave Breu a look of horror.

"I won't be gone long. Logan is a good man. I'll be back soon to get you," Breu whispered through her hair into her ear.

"Breu . . ." but he jumped off of the porch and onto the wagon.

"That's odd," Logan stated as he turned to go inside.

Aubrey stood there watching Breu leave, absolutely furious that he just left her stranded. Now Aubrey had no idea what to do or say.

To her relief Mr. Benton shouted, "Come on in. No sense in freezing out there when a fire's going."

Aubrey took in a deep breath, and entered the old shack.

Breu knew Aubrey was angry with him for what he just did, but he had to find Clara. Breu couldn't stand to see Aubrey suffer needlessly like she was, so he was about to find somebody who could talk some sense into her. He was certain that this would be Clara. The first place Breu was going to look was where Charles had been spending nearly all of his time, out at the Whitton place. If Clara wasn't there, then maybe Charles would be, and he could tell Breu where to find her.

He drove the wagon hastily, because he didn't want Aubrey to think that he broke his word and abandoned her there. Before long, Breu arrived at his destination, and to his relief Charles was working on the house. Once again Breu jumped off of the wagon after bringing it to a complete stop, but tried not to act too impatient.

"Hello Charles."

"Breu, just in time. I could use the extra pair of hands."

"I would love to stay and help you Charles, but I've got to find Clara. It's rather important."

Charles looked up from his work.

"Oh, is everything alright?"

"Yes, I've just got to talk to her about something."

"She's around back."

"Good."

As soon as Breu started walking, Charles spoke again.

"Hey Breu, you've got to tell me about you and the colonel."

"I will," Breu said, then he turned and began walking again.

He didn't mind telling Charles of what happened, but right now Breu had more important things to take care of. Breu was glad that Clara was here so he wouldn't have to keep searching. When he reached the back of the house, Breu saw Clara digging. He didn't know until he got next to her that she was digging up flowers that were buried in the snow.

"Hello Clara."

"Breu! How are you dear?"

"I'm fine Clara. Can I talk to you for a moment?"

"Of course," she replied straightening her stance and holding onto the handle of the shovel.

Breu took a moment and then began.

"We've got to do something about Aubrey. You see, she blames herself for Marty's suicide."

"What? Is that why she has been acting so strangely?"

"Well, there is more. I finally got her to admit that she not only blames herself, but she is convinced that you blame her as well." Clara was stunned and couldn't speak. "She thinks that if she had never come home, then Marty would still be alive. Aubrey especially feels guilt because you hadn't seen him in years . . ."

"I see," Clara interrupted.

"I thought I'd bring her by a little later so you can talk to her. I've tried, but it did no good."

"Yes, bring her. I didn't know she felt that way. I thought she was busy working and trying to focus on her career. I wondered why she hadn't spoken to us in a while."

"Aubrey is depressed, and she needs help."

"We'll get it straightened out Breu, thank you for letting me know."

Chapter 14

"Reconciliation"

B REU GOT BACK onto his wagon and headed right back to Mr. Benton's. After he arrived and knocked on the door, Breu didn't hear a sound. Not even the sound of their voices. Feeling at home now, instead of like a stranger as before, Breu opened the door and stepped inside, only to see the fire slowly dying within a large empty room that was growing cold.

"Where did they go?" Breu thought.

The only other place he could imagine that they would go was the gazebo. Before Breu left the shack, he called both Aubrey and Logan's names aloud, to make sure they really weren't there before he left. Only silence filled Breu's listening ears, so he shut the door behind him, and drove his wagon to the gazebo.

As he rode Breu couldn't help but think, "Logan hasn't gotten out of the house since I have known him. Maybe he will not only be good medicine for Aubrey, but possibly she will be good medicine for him."

Though Breu was almost certain the two he searched for would be at the gazebo, he would still be quite surprised to see Logan out of his old shack. Breu knew that Logan did leave every now and then to go visit Hannah's grave and fill the lanterns with oil, but Breu had never seen this with his own eyes. However, the evidence was there, because the lanterns that hung within the gazebo were always full of oil.

Sure enough at the end of Breu's journey, he saw Logan and Aubrey sitting in the gazebo together talking. He was stunned to actually see Aubrey smiling.

"Good," Breu thought, "maybe she's not mad."

The two noticed Breu as he slowly approached the gazebo, then Aubrey's smile faded.

"Safe trip?" Logan asked.

"Yes, I didn't go far." Aubrey looked away, and Breu found that his hopes of Aubrey not being upset that he left her had faded along with her rare smile. "Did you both have a good visit?"

"You need to bring Aubrey around more often. I really enjoyed this."

"I would love to come visit you more often," Aubrey replied to Logan with a smile.

Breu was glad that they both became acquainted and had a delightful visit.

"Well, I hate to run off again," Breu stated, "but I've got to be getting Aubrey back home. Would you like a ride?"

"No no. I make this trip all the time. See my trail?"

Breu looked and just as Logan said, there was a narrow but cleaned out trail in the woods leading back to his house. Logan and Aubrey stood, giving each other a hug and smile, then the three bid their goodbyes. Logan was already on his trail by the time Aubrey and Breu were on the wagon, and Aubrey watched the old man disappear into the woods until Breu changed the direction of the wagon. As they rode, Breu thought that he would begin an easy conversation.

"So what do you think about Logan?"

"He is the kind of person you can have a good time with, even if you are just sitting around talking. Logan is very gentlemanly and polite, considerate, and I can't help but somehow feel comfortable around him."

"Good."

"You shouldn't have left me there like that. I can't believe you did that."

Suddenly the mood of the conversation changed by Aubrey's reproof.

"But you said . . ."

"It doesn't matter Breu! I didn't know what kind of man he was when you left. How dare you treat me like that."

Breu couldn't believe what he was hearing and became defensive.

"Excuse me! Treat you! How about the way you've treated me huh? Don't you trust me enough to feel safe where I take you? Don't you trust me enough to believe me when I say you need to meet someone because he is a good man?"

Aubrey said nothing, because she had no answer. Finally one came to her.

"Yes I trust you Breu, to stay with me when you bring me to meet said person, and not leave me stranded!"

Both were furious with each other now, shouting when they spoke. Shortly they arrived at the Whitton's place and Aubrey became confused.

"I thought you said you were taking me home."

As Breu pulled the horses to a complete stop, Breu looked at Aubrey angrily.

"You are home."

Aubrey glared at him for a moment, and then climbed down from the wagon. She was taken by surprise when Breu snapped the reins and left. Breu had planned on staying at first, but after the fight with Aubrey, he just wanted to go back to the sheriff's office and get to work. He was sick of it all. Trying to help her, not being able to do anything right in her eyes, and hurting from her indifferent actions. Breu didn't want to give up on Aubrey, but he was getting to the point of accepting that maybe they just weren't meant to be.

Charles kept working, not giving any sort of sign that he was aware of Aubrey's presence. She didn't want to speak to him, and after looking at Charles, she finally noticed what he was now spending all of his time doing. The house was coming up beautifully though there hadn't been a great amount of progress. Aubrey figured that when she saw it, if she ever did, she would hate and despise it.

As she stood there staring at her family's future, Aubrey couldn't despise it. She wanted to, but couldn't. Clara walked around the beginnings of the house and saw Aubrey standing there.

"Aubrey! It's good to see you!" she said with happiness in her voice. The sound of her mother's voice surprised Aubrey as well, because she had not heard Clara speak like that since before Marty died. Clara set the shovel she had been using beside Charles, who did not look up from what he was doing.

"Let's go for a stroll," Clara said, and Aubrey recognized the direction they were heading. Clara was leading Aubrey to the meadow. "How do you like working for Dr. Starks?"

"I really enjoy it. I love tending to people. How are you doing?"

"Oh I'm doing wonderful," she replied with a smile.

"You are?" Aubrey asked in disbelief.

"Yes. Are you surprised?"

"Well, yes."

"Why?"

"Because every time I have seen you, we didn't even speak, and you always looked so down."

"I know now and I want to apologize to you for that Aubrey. Just because I lost one child doesn't give me the right to forget the other." Aubrey was shocked by her mother's words.

"So from what I understand Aubrey, you blame yourself for Marty's suicide." The words were easier to say for Clara now. "Not only because you feel guilty, but because you thought I blamed you too."

"Did Breu come see you?"

"A little while ago," Clara answered.

"So that's what he was up to," Aubrey thought. "Yes mama, that's how I feel, and my life has become a disaster," she willingly admitted.

"Aubrey, I want you to know that I have never blamed you for Marty's death, and I never will. You can't help the decisions someone else makes, and I thank God everyday that I still have you." Aubrey began to cry. "Now you need to stop feeling guilty for something that was out of your hands. Marty chose his lot in life, and it would not have mattered if you weren't on that train, because he probably would have done the same thing to somebody else. I'm not glad that he did what he did, but I am thankful that he died here at home by his own hand, than somewhere else by someone else's."

Immediately Aubrey began to fill a load lifted off of her shoulders, and God's love and mercy began to push out the guilt and blame.

"So you don't believe Marty died because of me?" Aubrey asked through tears.

"Honey, the only person who has died because of you is Jesus, and you know how that turned out."

All at the same time Aubrey felt an overflowing of love and conviction within her heart. Love because God and her family still loved her, and conviction with the way she had treated God and her family. Now that one matter was settled, another still remained.

"Why didn't someone tell me that papa was going to burn down the cabin?"

"He mostly did it because of me. I couldn't live in that house with Marty's blood stained on the floor. Your papa had been extremely busy moving things out that we wanted to keep, so he couldn't tell you Aubrey. The only other person who knew about it was me, and I didn't want to say a word until after it was done."

Now alot of Aubrey's anger against Charles diminished with Clara's explanation because Aubrey respected her decision. Aubrey was beginning to see the situation from Clara's point of view, and things made more sense now.

"So are you alright now?" Clara asked.

"I'm going to be. I'm glad we had this talk."

"Me too."

Without Aubrey even realizing it, they had been standing at the foot of Marty's grave. She looked down at Marty's resting place, and wasn't sure what to think.

"I'm going to head back now."

"I'll be there in a little bit. I want to stay here for a moment," Aubrey said.

Clara turned to leave, and Aubrey watched her until she disappeared. Once Clara was out of sight, Aubrey crossed her arms and stared down at the fresh grave. There were so many questions she wanted to know. Like what kind of person Marty was, why he left home, and why he abandoned his life and family for robbery.

Aubrey still had to forgive Marty. She had already forgiven him for kidnapping and putting her life in danger, but now she had to forgive Marty for not being apart of her life, and worse, obviously not wanting to be. Aubrey fell onto her knees and closed her eyes. A slight breeze blew on her, and Aubrey could sense spring in the air.

Tears began to fall freely in the privacy of the meadow. It was such a peaceful beautiful place. There was something that Aubrey needed to do, something she had not done in a while now. Aubrey slowly and tearfully began to pray. She thanked God for His patience with her, and for Clara not blaming her for Marty's death. Aubrey asked forgiveness for the way she had been living, and for the help and strength to forgive Marty, and her papa for what he had said to her.

Having sat there for so long on her knees, Aubrey's legs were going numb. The cold from the snow was touching Aubrey's skin through her dress making her cold, but she didn't care about any of these things. Aubrey just kept her eyes closed while tears still fell, and soaked in this overdue fellowship with the Heavenly Father. Aubrey was broken, and now had to rely solely on God's strength, instead of her own, to get pieced back together.

So much had happened, and God was there the entire time though Aubrey felt forgotten. While Aubrey believed that Clara and Charles were not getting through this very well, the truth was that Aubrey was handling the situation worse than anyone.

She opened her eyes, wiping all of her tears away. Aubrey now felt renewed, revived, forgiven. She laid all of her burdens on the Lord, and would have to work one day at a time on leaving them there. Aubrey stood to her feet trying to keep a steady balance because her legs were numb. After a short while, Aubrey gave Marty's grave one last look, then began making her way through the snow back to the Whitton's new house.

Chapter 15

"Pie"

A S AUBREY WALKED back, she realized that she could no longer keep giving Charles the silent treatment. Their relationship needed mending as well. Aubrey finally made it back and approached Charles. He didn't look up, but Aubrey wasn't going to wait until he made eye contact with her.

"Why did you tell me that the house burning down was none of my concern?"

Her voice was respectful yet firm. Charles looked up after realizing that Aubrey was talking to him. Clara stood by Charles and was made curious by Aubrey's question.

"Is that what you're so upset about?"

"How could I not be? I grew up in that house. I had memories in there. I understand now why you did it, but I want to know why you said it was none of my concern."

Clara then stared at her husband waiting for his answer, because she was unaware of what Charles had said to Aubrey. Charles exhaled heavily.

"I didn't mean that in an uncaring way. I only meant that soon you and Breu would be together, married and living in your own house on your own place getting on with your lives. We have to do the same. I knew if I told you before I burned it down, then you would probably throw a fit. We're ready for a good change Aubrey, and I knew you wouldn't be living here much longer."

"Well you didn't have to say it like that. I'm not a child anymore, and you could have explained sooner."

"Look, I'm sorry I upset you, but you were busy and I was getting busy . . ."

"From now on all of us need to stop what we're doing long enough to make what's wrong right," Clara interrupted prudently.

"It's all over with now. Let's just put everything behind us and start fresh," Charles finished.

He and Aubrey's relationship had just been strangely restored, but Charles didn't believe in dwelling on things that bothered him. In his stable mind Charles felt that if something is broken, then you fix it and move on just like that. While this was easy for him, Aubrey had not inherited this trait. She forgave Charles with God's help, but it would take a little longer for the hurt to go away. However, anytime Aubrey and Charles had a spat, including this one, she would move on just as he did, but reluctantly though Aubrey respected Charles enough not to keep bringing up the subject.

The Whittons did not stay too much longer at their home place because Charles and Clara were both tired and wanted to go back to the hotel and rest. Aubrey rode back with them in their wagon, feeling so much better than she had in weeks. How long had she needlessly suffered, all because she would not trust in the Lord! Aubrey thanked Him again in her heart for His love and mercy, and as she rode into town with her family, it was as if Aubrey was a new woman.

All of a sudden the air seemed fresh in her nostrils, the white snow became a delight instead of a nuisance, and the town of Moline felt like home instead of a strange place where Aubrey couldn't fit in. Her outlook on life completely changed from one of sorrow and hopelessness, to one of strength, comfort, and optimism. Aubrey's life was back, restored by the only person who could perform such a miracle, God.

There was still someone Aubrey had to get right with, who she had mistreated and pushed away for no good reason. Breu was her one true love, and Aubrey now had to restore their relationship before she lost him forever. Aubrey felt so wretched with how she had treated Breu, and wouldn't blame him if he never took her back, and that possibility brought tears to her eyes.

Aubrey couldn't just walk into the sheriff's office and start apologizing. She wanted to do something special for him, and she knew just what to do. After getting out of the wagon, Aubrey said goodbye to her parents until next time, then went into Esther's. Aubrey was relieved and thankful that Esther had all of the ingredients to make a pecan pie, which she knew from her past experience to be Breu's favorite.

He would enjoy seeing her come in with his favorite dessert Aubrey was sure of, after all, she had always heard that the way into a man's heart was through his stomach. Whether this was true or not, Aubrey was soon to find out. Carefully and profusely she blended in the ingredients.

"You making something child?" Esther asked as she came into her room for a moment.

"I'm making a pie for Breu. I hope you don't mind."

"No child, but what does this mean considering that you two are no longer engaged?"

"It means that I've been a persistent idiot, and I'm hoping he will forgive me. Pecan pie is his favorite."

Esther only smiled, happy that Aubrey finally after all this time came to her senses. She went back into the store, leaving Aubrey to wrap herself up in preparation of the pie, and the hope that Breu would take her back. Anxiousness was growing worse with each minute that slowly passed by. Aubrey would sometimes think, "What if he isn't there and I don't get to see him again today?"

However she remembered that Breu lived in the jailhouse, and he wasn't leaving for any trips that she knew of, so where else could he be? Aubrey had to trust that Breu would be there and stop worrying, which was very difficult indeed.

Preparing the pie didn't take as long as it seemed, but finally the pie was finished baking, and though Aubrey was ready to go now, she had to let it cool down a little bit. To help keep her mind off of the time Aubrey decided to go into the store. Esther was piddling behind the counter, and Aubrey somehow got caught up into looking through the windows at the people who passed by.

Without paying attention to where she was going, Aubrey was slowly walking to the back of the store. She didn't even notice who was standing in the back of the store until she nearly ran into her. Aubrey was surprised to see Rose Bennett, and the shock of almost running into her could easily be seen on Aubrey's countenance.

"Rose," Aubrey said.

"Aubrey," Rose replied slowly and slyly. "Is it true that you have been conversing with my son and engaging him in private matters?"

Aubrey was completely taken off guard.

"Excuse me?" was all she could manage to say.

"My son has a special future ahead of him and should not be distracted by a homeless unfortunate soul such as you."

Aubrey didn't know what to think!

"If I find that you are still trying to coerce my son into falling for a mere poor excuse for a young lady, then I will not be so nice the next time we meet again."

"Rose . . ."

"It is Mrs. Bennett," she sternly corrected.

"I am not coercing your son to do anything, and you will not speak to me in that manner. You will treat me with respect Rose."

Aubrey was furious.

"Stay away from my son," Rose snapped before she walked away.

All Aubrey could do was stand there in disbelief.

"Does Rose think that Ethan is in love with me?" she thought. "Where could she possibly have come up with that notion?"

Aubrey was sick of Rose Bennett's mouth, because of her arrogant disdain for people who were no less than she, and because of her attacks on the Whittons. Ethan was in no way in love with Aubrey but if he were, Aubrey was a well respected person in Moline, the kind of girl any mother would want their son to be with, save for Rose Bennett. No young lady would ever be good enough for Ethan in Rose's mind, which made Ethan dread the day he would reveal his secret love to his mother.

Turning around to go back into Esther's room, Aubrey didn't care if the pecan pie was cool or not, she was ready to go see Breu. By the time she stepped out into the cold atmosphere with the pie in hand, the sun was sinking in the west. The day passed by quickly, but it was very eventful for Aubrey. Across and down the street she went until she got to the jailhouse.

Without knocking on the door Aubrey walked inside. Upon entering she saw nothing, but heard someone shutting one of the cells. Then Breu came into the main room where Aubrey stood, being unaware that she had come in, and amazed to see her presence. They both stood there for a moment just glaring at each other, waiting for something to appear in their head so they could use that to start a conversation.

As Breu walked over to his desk Aubrey said, "Breu, thank you for taking me to Mr. Benton's and my parents' place. I can't describe how sorry I am for the way I've treated you and how selfish I have acted. All I can say is I am so sorry."

Breu listened.

"Instead of pushing you away I should have clung to you, and I don't blame you for not taking me back, but Breu, I want to marry you. I love you."

She had tried to be strong while she made her apology, but tears couldn't be hindered nor her voice smooth instead of shaky. Breu sighed heavily with great relief. God had answered his persistent prayer.

"What have you got there?" he asked as he moved close to Aubrey.

"Oh, I made you a pecan pie just now so it's fresh. I knew it was your favorite."

She held the pie out to him, hoping that soon he would express his forgiveness, if he had forgiven her. Breu took the pie and set it aside. He moved closer to Aubrey until he was staring down into her face. His strong hands caressed her cheeks and hair, then suddenly Aubrey realized that Breu was expressing his forgiveness without words.

"So you'll marry me?" he asked one last time.

"If you still want me to," she softly replied, being so entranced by his touch.

He leaned down and passionately kissed her, while thanking God the entire time that He had worked everything out. Aubrey had spent so much time away from Breu that she didn't want to leave the jailhouse. She stayed with Breu, and they both caught up on time that was lost between them while sharing pieces of pecan pie.

They talked and talked, and Aubrey even shared with her once again future husband, of the confrontation she and Rose had before she came to him.

Breu shook his head and stated, "That woman."

"So I guess she believes that Ethan is in love with me, when really his love is for Tonya Woods."

"I can't figure out why she would think that," Breu replied.

"Me either. The only kindness Ethan has shown me was when he brought me the jewelry box he made and a bouquet of camellias. Other than that I haven't even spoke to him."

"He made you a jewelry box?"

"Yes, but it was an apologetic gesture, kind of like this pie. Ethan gave it to me when he apologized for the way he acted that day."

"I see. He came over and apologized to me too."

Breu did not mention to Aubrey about the note Ethan let him read. Though it seemed very out of the ordinary, and quite chilling for that matter, since he had heard nothing more of the situation Breu figured that it must have been some sort of joke, therefore he did not deem it necessary to mention the note to Aubrey.

Before they knew it, darkness covered Moline, and though Aubrey and Breu were reluctant for her to go, she kissed Breu goodbye and left. Both Aubrey and Breu felt better tonight than they had in a couple of months, which could easily be seen on their countenances. As Aubrey walked through the twilight snow-covered street, someone ran up beside her.

AMAZING GRACE WILLIAMS

"Tonya?" Aubrey said surprised.

"Hello Aubrey. I can't be gone long," she informed very out of breath. "Mama doesn't know I'm not in my room."

"Tonya, why did you sneak out?" Aubrey asked, afraid of Tonya getting caught.

"Oh I know I shouldn't have, but I had to know if Ethan apologized to you. I haven't been able to see him, and to be honest it's driving me mad."

"He did apologize but, why haven't you been able to see him? Did your mother find out?"

Tonya realized she had said too much. She was told by Ethan not to let anyone know about the note and the danger that both of them could possibly be in.

"Oh she doesn't know," she quickly replied, "but you understand how difficult it must be for us to sneak around without being found out. We are just trying to be cautious."

Tonya formed a smile on her face though Aubrey could hardly see it and continued.

"Well I need to be getting back Aubrey. I just wanted to make sure Ethan did apologize."

"He did, but Tonya you shouldn't be riding alone all by yourself. It is dangerous."

"I know, and I won't do it again, but this has been on my mind heavily and I haven't had the chance to speak with you before."

"Just be careful," Aubrey commanded.

"I will. Goodnight Aubrey."

Tonya hurriedly ran down the street to where her horse quietly stood, jumped on his back, and galloped toward home. She was a very sweet girl, never showing any disrespect to anyone. Tonya was very agreeable with a timid nature, and Aubrey hoped she would not encounter any trouble along the way home.

Esther was sitting by the fire as usual, reading one of her many books. Aubrey sighed merrily and contently as she hung up her jacket. She joined Esther next to the fire, staring into the fierce flames, but they did not produce any sort of fear because Aubrey was of a joyful spirit. Esther laid her book aside, and wanted to know how Aubrey had been faring all week since they had not conversed very much.

For the first time since Aubrey had been residing with her, Esther saw her smiling and joyful. This was the Aubrey Esther knew and missed, and now Esther thanked God, just as Breu had, for working this miracle in her life. They sat there by the fire, enjoying the warm ambience as both women talked, giggled, and even laughed.

Things were getting back to normal as the long winter's snow slowly began to melt with the coming of spring. Aubrey was able to enjoy working for Dr. Starks more now, though she still had her suspicions of him being a male-chauvinist. She missed Breu terribly during the day while she worked, even with him being only down the street. Aubrey visited her family often, and Clara seemed to be back to her normal personality as well.

Rose and Ingrid were still very faithful in church, with their gossip sessions never lacking in intensity, howbeit Rose had not spoken another word to Aubrey. Her son however spoke civilly to Aubrey every time he saw her, and she returned his kind act of civility, not caring if Rose saw or not. Tonya had obviously made it safely home the night she snuck into town to privately speak with Aubrey, because the next time Aubrey saw her she seemed unharmed and as merry as ever, which gave Aubrey the inclination that she wasn't caught out of her room that night.

Ethan still could not come up with an explanation to the note he found in the hollow of the tree, but a while had passed and no other notes had been left there. He then assumed that it was safe to continue on communicating to Tonya through the tree since absolutely nothing else strange had happened. Ethan was particularly cautious however in making sure that future notes could not be seen from either house, due to him almost being found out by his mother. Whoever had left the note that day was obviously wanting it to be found by either Tonya or Ethan, but he wanted to be extra careful anyway because them getting caught came too close before.

He informed Tonya of their restored communication line one Sunday afternoon when church services ended.

As Ethan had done before, he snuck up behind Tonya casually and in her ear said, "Go to the tree."

That was all he really had time to say, but he trusted that Tonya would do what he said without needing an explanation. Rose Bennett had not told Ethan about her confronting Aubrey that day in Esther's store, but ever since Ingrid had informed Rose of Ethan's love for Aubrey, she was absolutely convinced that Aubrey was luring her perfect son away from his good senses. Ethan knew nothing of the matter, but kept meeting with Tonya Woods in the forest whenever his time would allow.

Breu took Aubrey to see Mr. Benton more often, which both of them thoroughly enjoyed. She became close to Logan, seeing him as a sort of grandfather figure she never had. During slow times in the doctor's office, Aubrey began doodling, drawing, and making plans for her future home, and after revising a few times would take her sketches to Breu to get his opinion on her ideas, which most of the time he approved of.

Ella, Deputy Kevin's wife, was showing dramatically with the expectance of their new baby arriving sometime in summer. In Aubrey's eyes, everything had gotten back to the way it should be. She could tell that her faith was getting stronger each day, and somehow through everything she had been through, her relationship with the Lord had grown more dependent and closer than it was before.

Now that Aubrey was away from Charles and Clara all of the time, she became her own strong independent woman, who took more time to focus on her Christian life and how to make it better. One day as she was counting her blessings in Dr. Starks' office, the realization made itself clear to her.

"I couldn't be pieced together until I was broken, and that is the only kind of person God will work with."

Chapter 16

"House Calls"

SPRING FINALLY MADE its appearance by melting all of the
snow, and Aubrey ardently loved this time of year. The days were
the perfect temperature, the sky was a beautiful bright blue, and all of the
flowers that had been peacefully sleeping under the cold snow, rose out of
the ground in great vibrancy.

The two houses were coming along promptly, though Breu's still lagged
behind in speed. On Aubrey's time off from working she would go over to
the hotel, unless Clara walked to Esther's store, and sew with her mother.
Without having to solely rely on Charles' money now, Aubrey was capable
of buying her own material and other items she needed to furnish her new
home with after it was built and she was married. These times with Clara
brought them closer, and both women were able to easily express to the
other of their plans for the future.

"Have you set a date?" Clara asked her daughter as they sat in Esther's
store one bright spring day.

"We haven't really discussed it. I know Breu has to finish the house
before we can marry, but neither of us really know when that will be."

So the date was still unsettled, but Aubrey was in no hurry because she
wanted to allow her wedding day to be perfect and not rushed. Since Breu
busied himself when he could with the building of their house, Aubrey
busied herself with the furnishings.

One afternoon when the doctor's office hadn't been busy, Dr. Starks
stated, "I need to go pay a visit to the Bridges home."

Without having rehearsed it or even thinking about it, Aubrey surprised
herself when she asked, "Dr. Starks, why am I not allowed to go on house
calls? Is it because you believe that women belong in the office?"

Dr. Starks was confused and completely taken off guard.

"You are allowed," he informed wondering what all of this was about.
"I thought you didn't want to go on house calls. You are welcome to go
anytime Aubrey."

"So you don't think that I need to stay in here because I am a woman?"

"Now where did you come up with an idea like that?" he asked before placing his hands on his hips.

Aubrey wasn't quite sure if she should reveal the name of the man who planted this notion, but there was no way around it now. She had to explain.

"Well," she began, "I hope I don't upset you by saying it was Jim who told me that. To be honest, he acted very sexist around me while he was here and I assumed that you were the same."

"Huh," Dr. Starks replied. "I believe a woman has every right to go on house calls and work just as any man, and yes, I know my son is a sexist but he didn't get it from me."

Aubrey couldn't believe she just expressed her feelings like that, especially since they were negative about his own son, but she was relieved to see that Dr. Starks did not get upset about her honesty.

"I'll explain everything on the way," he said as he held the door open for her to walk through, so Aubrey went first and Dr. Starks helped her onto the wagon.

"So he really isn't male-chauvinist like Jim," Aubrey thought as the doctor snapped the horse's reins. "I have been completely wrong about him."

"I couldn't raise Jim on my own when my wife died, so he obviously has been under the influence of his uncle. Had I been leading him most of his life, he would not be the way he is toward women."

"I see," Aubrey replied as they rode along the dirt road. "Well then I owe you an apology Dr. Starks. I shouldn't have made assumptions about you based on the behavior of your son. I am sorry."

Dr. Starks smiled.

"It's quite alright Aubrey. It is only natural to think of someone's actions as being a result of the leadership of one's parents. Though not true in some cases, Jim is a result of his uncle's leadership. I reprove him when need be, however to change his mind set about females entirely is too late. I never have cared for his uncle's attitude toward women, but I allowed him guardianship of Jim so there is nothing I can do about it now."

"I understand. Yet I would think that since he is from the city he would be more evolved. Especially since more women are employed there than here."

"One would consider that but in Jim's case, he seems to hold onto the morals he was taught as a child, one of which is that women are inferior."

"I believe that men are much stronger than women and are more capable physically, as well as being the head of the home, but for women to be restricted from places and activities just because they are of the weaker gender is hardly what God had in mind I think," Aubrey stated very surely. "I can't stand it when a man thinks less of a woman just because she is the weaker sex. Just because someone is weaker doesn't mean they are lesser."

"I agree," Dr. Starks said with a nod of his head. "Who knows," he continued with a chuckle, "maybe one day women will have the right to vote!"

"Wouldn't that be something!" Aubrey replied chuckling as well. "I don't know if that will ever happen!"

After they both had a nice little laugh, Dr. Starks became serious again.

"But honestly Aubrey, if ever you desire to do something in my office, just let me know and I'll try to accommodate you. To tell you the truth, I'm rather glad to hear that you would like to start accompanying me on house calls. As my face obviously shows, I am getting alot older, and I've noticed that it takes energy that I need in the office out of me. There should be someone in town at all times in case there is an emergency, after all the situation could turn fatal should I be gone, so why don't you come along with me a few more times until you become more acquainted with the patients I call on out here, and then I can stay in town with plenty of energy, and you can take full control of the house calls. How does that sound to you?"

"Oh I don't know Doctor, do you think that would be alright?"

"Well of course I do! I don't see anything wrong with it, and if you ask me the idea is genius because if ever there are problems outside of town, then you can inform Breu. You could be sort of like a spy!"

Aubrey chuckled at the Doctor's excitement but said, "Oh gosh Doctor, I see what you are saying but . . ."

"This decision is completely up to you Aubrey. I don't want you to feel pressured in any way, but I have been thinking lately of training someone I know I and my patients can trust, to go on the house calls for me. They do tire me out. If you would like to do what I have suggested but don't feel comfortable about going alone, then perhaps I could hire someone, of your choosing of course, to go along with you. These are just some things to be thinking about, and should you decide not to take this commission, do let me know soon so I can begin training someone. I've convinced myself that is what I should do, because that is all I can do."

"I really appreciate this Doctor. Give me a few days to decide because I need to discuss the matter with Breu. If he doesn't mind me traveling very far, then I would be happy to take your place. Being the sheriff and all, I suppose he knows your patients anyway. I don't see why he would object, but I must still bring up the subject to him."

"Good good," was the doctor's reply, and the Bridges cabin came in sight.

They traveled the rest of the way in silence. The cabin was in a lovely spot surrounded by weeping willow trees, yet sat there in complete seclusion from any other houses. Aubrey had always heard of the Bridges family, but had never actually met them. She knew that they were a couple in their forties who did not attend church due to Mr. Bridges and their son's health. Mr. Bridges was a sickly man who always seemed to catch whatever illness was making its way through the county, who was weak, and totally dependent on his wife. The son who lived with them was in his early twenties, but was mentally impaired from birth.

As Dr. Starks brought the wagon to a stop about twenty feet from the cabin he said, "I don't usually come here but maybe twice a month. There won't be a need for you to call on this house, unless you just feel that it is necessary. Mrs. Bridges takes very good care of her husband. Why don't you stay out here while I go inside. It won't take but a few minutes."

Dr. Starks got down from the wagon, leaving Aubrey to wait on his return. After he went into the cabin, Aubrey looked out over the fresh landscape. As she admired the bright plentiful flowers the ground produced, Aubrey felt her heart leap out of her chest when she heard someone shooting a shotgun and screaming. Out of reflex Aubrey grabbed onto the seat of the wagon, but the shooting still loudly banged making the horses jump and fuss.

Before Aubrey could grab the reins, the wagon was racing through the fields dodging trees on the right and left. Aubrey was still holding onto the seat of the wagon because there was no hope of being able to catch the reins. They had fallen and were dragging on the ground underneath the wagon. All Aubrey could do was scream and hang on for dear life as the wagon sped through the flowers she had just admired, trying not to bounce out of the seat. It was difficult to stay on because the wagon kept trying to flip over.

At one point during this horrendous ride, the horses ran the wagon over some stumps sticking out of the ground, causing Aubrey to fall down into the floor of the wagon. She stared death in the face before she was able to grab the seat and barely pick herself up. Aubrey had to jump, but there were too many trees. To jump right now would be suicide.

"Jesus help me!" she cried.

The horses were somehow missing the many trees that surrounded them, by divine intervention Aubrey knew, but to her great horror the horses ran too close beside one of the trees hitting it, and it knocked Aubrey off of the wagon with a hard hit. She screamed at the top of her lungs, out of pure fright this time instead of trying to gain someone's attention, and Aubrey landed heavily on the ground rolling in the thick grass and weeds until she came to a complete stop.

The horses had gotten detached from the doctor's wagon due to the hard blow of the tree, and they eventually ceased their escape a quarter of a mile from where Aubrey lay. The wagon lay near Aubrey on its side with two wheels still turning, evidence that the accident had just happened.

After the world seemed to stop spinning, Aubrey opened her eyes to see herself buried in grass and greenery. She feared the pain she would soon feel but tried to carefully move each of her limbs to see if anything was broken. Moving one limb at a time, Aubrey was thankful to find that nothing was broken, atleast to her knowledge at the moment. Pain seared through her whole body however, and instead of trying to get up just yet, Aubrey laid there in the tall grass, slowly catching her breath.

A few minutes later, finally having the ability to breathe at a normal pace, Aubrey tried to raise herself into a sitting position. Her attempt was a success, but Aubrey felt like she had just been beaten. She shook, and as she looked around Aubrey noticed that her fall had barely allowed her to miss a tree. Aubrey thanked God for sparing her life. Checking out her arms and legs she found many cuts and scrapes, nothing too serious, but Aubrey knew that was a miracle from God as well because she should have at least had a broken bone if not died, though Aubrey was grateful to God for sparing her from excruciating pain as well as death.

Not being sure of what exactly just happened, Aubrey shakily yet slowly stood to her feet. She began walking back the way the wagon just came following its faint tracks left behind in the fields, because Aubrey wasn't sure if anyone, especially Dr. Starks, could find her. It was a slow and painful go, but Aubrey took her time trying not to collapse along the way.

As soon as the gunshots were fired Dr. Starks ran outside only to see the wagon take off in a fury with Aubrey still on. Without even asking, he found a horse the Bridges family owned, and instead of following the wagon and Aubrey, he galloped back into town to get Breu. He did not know what the outcome might be, so he had to get help before he tried to chase down the wagon.

Though Dr. Starks tried to remain calm as the horse galloped, he could not dispose of the worry that overcame him. It did not take long to get back into town as when he left, one reason was because he galloped, and two because he wasn't dragging a wagon behind him. The elderly doctor had not ridden a horse like that in many years, and was surprised he had not killed himself in the process of trying to get help, but he knew he would pay for his actions later. Right now Aubrey was his only concern, so he hurriedly yet wisely got down from the horse once he reached the jailhouse and busted through the door. Kevin and Breu looked up in alarm when the door swung open and Doctor Starks stood there breathing heavily.

"My wagon took off with Aubrey on it. She might be hurt. Come quick!" the doctor shouted.

Breu jumped to his feet, as did Deputy Kevin, and as they ran outside to get onto their horses Breu asked, "Where?"

"The Bridges place headed south," Doctor Starks answered.

Without anymore questions Kevin and Breu took off, leaving Doctor Starks trailing behind. Breu couldn't imagine what happened, but he would find that out later. Aubrey was what consumed his mind as he and Kevin galloped. They both knew where the Bridges property was, so it did not take long for the two to arrive and immediately spot the wagon's tracks.

Breu and Kevin kept a steady pace as they followed the wagon's tracks, and before long they saw a figure in a dress lagging through the field. Breu's heart leaped when he realized it was Aubrey, because now he knew that she was definitely alive and obviously able enough to walk.

Aubrey felt such relief when she saw Breu and Kevin galloping toward her. She stopped trying to walk and just stood there, waiting for Breu to reach her. When he finally did, he jumped off of his horse before it even stopped and ran to Aubrey, putting his hands on her shoulders. He immediately began checking her out for serious injuries, but like Aubrey, only saw cuts and scrapes which was a relief to him.

"Are you alright?" he asked with fear in his eyes.

"I think so. I don't believe anything's broken, but I'm hurting all over."

Breu picked her up and set her on his horse, then got on right behind her.

"Where's the wagon?" he asked.

She pointed in the direction where it lay, and without Breu having to give Kevin any orders, Kevin took off in a gallop once more following the tracks so he could retrieve the wagon. Breu snapped the reins on his horse, and the horse ran back toward Moline, not in a speed he had just run, but instead a slower gallop.

Aubrey was hurting and felt her whole body throb with each stomp the horse's hoofs made on the ground. Again this brought back the memory of when she was held hostage, but atleast she was in the arms of her lover, instead of a half-crazed brother. Either way Aubrey was ready to be off of the horse and lying down in Esther's bed. She tried to endure the ride back into town, but it was very difficult.

Breu heard her grunt and groan at times, and kept trying to comfort her by saying, "We're almost there love."

Before arriving back in Moline, Breu met Dr. Starks who was so happy and relieved to see Aubrey alive and not seriously injured.

Stopping only long enough to say "We're going to your office," Breu kept going and Dr. Starks followed on behind, trying his best not to give out. When the three got to the doctor's office Breu would not let Aubrey walk, but instead carried her in his arms.

Aubrey became disappointed after Breu informed Dr. Starks of where they were going, because she was hoping to just be taken to Esther's where she could rest.

As Breu carried her into Dr. Starks office she said, "I really don't think this is necessary Breu. Nothing is broken."

"I want to be sure," he replied in a tone of voice that told Aubrey he wasn't going to change his mind.

Aubrey was too tired and sore to argue, so she gave in hoping that the exam wouldn't take very long. Poor Dr. Starks shook and breathed heavily from all of his adrenaline pumping, and all of the riding. Breu sat Aubrey on the table once inside the office, and Dr. Starks carefully began the examination.

"What happened?" Breu asked while the doctor worked.

"That Bridges boy," he said. "They keep their guns hidden from him, but somehow he found one. He ran outside screaming and shooting in a crazed rant, which of course scared the horses."

Everything now made since to Aubrey, but Breu was very upset about the whole ordeal. If the Bridges son wasn't lunatic, then Breu would not hesitate to arrest him and bring him to jail, but because of the state he was in, Breu knew that would do no good. Breu even had a good mind to go back and give the Bridges a good talking to, but he was also aware that Mrs. Bridges was doing the best she could by herself taking care of her husband and son.

After Dr. Starks explained what happened, Aubrey realized just how dangerous the Bridges son could be. She wasn't sure just how mentally impaired he was, but she found out today that it could be to a fatal degree. Breu was so angry, but tried to remain calm because he understood that if the boy was in his right mind, then he would not have put Aubrey in such danger.

It was all just an accident that thankfully didn't kill anybody, but if it had, then Breu would have had to bring the young man to jail. After the examination Dr. Starks let out a heavy sigh and assured Aubrey and Breu that she would suffer from unpleasant soreness for a while, but other than that she was fine.

Aubrey really didn't want Breu carrying her through town back to Esther's, because of the curious countenances and endless stares of everyone who would see them walk by, but Aubrey knew that there was no point in arguing, and she really only had the strength to relax in his arms. It felt so wonderful on her aching body to lie down on Esther's bed, and Breu had to explain what happened to Esther. She was shocked, and promised Breu that she would definitely keep her eye on Aubrey.

He did however stay a while with Aubrey, having pulled up Esther's rocking chair beside the bed, until Aubrey fell asleep. Being in a state of unconsciousness, Aubrey didn't even know that Breu gently kissed her lips before going back to his office. Dr. Starks was entirely worn out and had to go lay down as well. Though he said nothing about it to her, Dr. Starks didn't expect Aubrey to come back to work in a few days, or until she felt like it. Kevin managed to gather the horses, pull the wagon back into its proper stance, connect the two back together, tie his own horse to the back of the wagon, and then finally ride into Moline.

After getting the wagon to the doctor's office and untying his own horse, Kevin jumped on its back and grabbed the reins of the Bridges horse so he could return it to its rightful owner. Deputy Kevin had stayed busy after Aubrey's accident, but finally finished his duties before the day was done. Breu was exceptionally grateful to Kevin for getting all of that done.

By the time he returned home to Ella and his young children, Kevin was ready for rest just as Dr. Starks had been.

Aubrey awoke for a little while when Breu came to check on her just before nightfall, and had no problem falling back to sleep when he left. She did not dream, but did hurt every time she rolled, which did not occur much during the night. Mrs. Bridges found a new place to hide their guns, and felt horrified by what had happened to Aubrey, even though she didn't know the young girl. Mrs. Bridges felt responsible for her son's actions, just as she had all of his life.

Once Rose Bennett found out about the incident she scorned the Bridges son for his handicap, even though it wasn't his fault because he was born that way, and she spoke harshly of the Bridges for not having put him in some sort of asylum. She said these cruel judgmental comments to anyone who would listen whenever she came into town, and though most didn't agree with her, Ingrid fueled her gossipy fire.

Chapter 17

"Henry Worthington"

IT TOOK A week for Aubrey's soreness and the doctor's exhaustion to go away. Once their ailments had past however, both were as good as new. Aubrey didn't want to ask Breu whether or not he approved of her going on house calls alone until she was healed. To ask him for an answer when she lay on Esther's bed in pain would be ludicrous. Aubrey did want to go on house calls so she could spend more time outside of the office, so one Friday afternoon while they were spending time together, Aubrey gathered all of her courage and asked.

"Breu, Dr. Starks is getting very elderly as you can obviously see, and he needs someone to start taking house calls in his stead. He offered me the job."

She heard Breu grunt and saw doubt with negativity cover his face. "Do you want to go on house calls?" he asked.

"I've thought about it, and I would really enjoy it I think. He isn't pressuring me at all if that is what you're concerned about."

"No it's not that, I don't feel comfortable with you going off alone, especially after what recently happened."

Aubrey was afraid that Breu was going to bring up the accident in this particular conversation, but she really couldn't blame him for it because she most probably would have done the same.

"Dr. Starks said that if I didn't want to go alone then I could choose someone to go along with me. He will hire them."

That sounded a little better to Breu, but he didn't show any sign of gladness.

"Let me think about it," he finally answered to Aubrey's disappointment.

Though that was Breu's answer he did not necessarily mean, "Let me think about whether or not to let you take the job," but without saying it he meant, "Let me think of someone trustworthy enough to go with you."

Breu wasn't going to allow Aubrey to go on house calls all by herself, and he kept this fact hidden from her for now, but from the moment she told him of her desire Breu's mind immediately began thinking, going through each female in town he knew to decide if she would make a good enough companion for Aubrey on these ventures. Breu did not think it appropriate for a male to accompany Aubrey.

"Is there anyone in particular you would want to go with you?" Breu asked since no one special came to mind.

"To be honest, I was leaning more toward Tonya Woods. She is a lovely kind girl, trustworthy, capable, and I am sure she would love a chance to be out of the house. Tonya takes directions and orders very well, and she has one of the most cheerful spirits I have ever seen."

"That sounds good. Tonya would make a helpful companion."

"So it's settled then?" Aubrey asked with excitement in her voice.

"Hold on a minute," Breu replied, "you haven't asked her yet."

"Oh I'm certain she'll agree."

"But still, you need to make sure she and her family are alright with this before you give Dr. Starks a final answer," he cautioned prudently.

The next Sunday morning during the sermon, Aubrey was so anxious to ask Tonya for her much needed services that she was about to go mad with excitement. Finally the service ended, and Aubrey got her chance. Aubrey's relationship with the Woods family remained in much better condition than she and Rose Bennett's. Though not as arrogant and disdainful as her nemesis Rose, Laura was very strict on her children, giving Aubrey the impression that she would not allow Tonya out of the house.

To Aubrey's, and now Tonya's great shock and happiness, Laura Woods agreed to allow her eldest daughter to work for Dr. Starks, under the condition that she return home at a certain time every evening, because obviously she still had chores to do at home. Now that Tonya was employed, all she could dwell on was putting her money up and saving it to help achieve her future plans with Ethan Bennett.

Tonya was excited about being employed and couldn't wait to start. When Ethan found out about it he was happy for Tonya and tried to figure when and how he would be able to see her without being found out. Everything worked out wonderfully for Aubrey and Tonya, and they became very good friends as they began working together.

"Do you know where papa put my bible?" Aubrey asked Clara one Friday.

Charles was in the supply store buying more supplies, and Aubrey was visiting her mother at the hotel.

"I don't know how much longer I can keep using Esther's old bible. It's very worn and fragile. I know she's letting me use it out of kindness, but it seems to be some kind of keepsake."

"I'm sure it's in here somewhere," Clara answered.

"Oh by the way, you wouldn't happen to know who Henry Worthington is do you?" Aubrey asked innocently.

Clara thought this question to be odd.

"Yes I knew him," she replied. "Henry Worthington was my papa."

Aubrey's world came to a halt as her jaw dropped open and she stared at her mother. Aubrey had never before been told about her grandparents on either side, and though she had been curious before, she never asked any questions. Aubrey always figured that if her mother and papa ever wanted her to know about them then they would say something, but they never did. This was the first time Aubrey had ever heard her maternal grandfather's name.

"What's wrong?" Clara asked as she saw the shock on Aubrey's countenance.

"Uh, I, I just remembered something back at Esther's mama. I'll be back."

Clara thought Aubrey was acting strange all of a sudden, but before she could ask any more questions Aubrey was out of the door. As Aubrey hurried back to Esther's, questions were flooding her mind.

"Why does Esther have my grandfather's bible?" was the main question she needed answered now.

Before, Aubrey had dropped the subject with Esther, because she had no idea who Henry Worthington was and she figured it to be none of her business.

However, she just found out that Henry was her grandfather, so Aubrey now believed that what Esther hid was her business. There was no anger toward Esther, but Aubrey had to find out the truth.

As she walked into the store Esther was helping a few customers, and once to her Aubrey quietly said, "I need to speak with you in private when you are done."

Without waiting for an answer Aubrey went into Esther's room and grabbed the bible. Aubrey waited patiently for Esther to join her, then finally after five minutes and getting the customers assisted, Esther came into the bedroom and saw Aubrey holding her old worn bible with Henry Worthington's name being displayed out in the open.

"Is this my grandfather's bible Esther?" Aubrey asked calmly but desiring honesty.

Esther sighed, realizing that she could keep her secret hidden no more.

"Yes. How did you find out?"

"I asked mama."

"You didn't tell her about the bible did you?"

"No, but what does it matter? What are you hiding?"

Esther still wanted to cling to what she had held in her heart for so long, but the time had come as she always feared, to reveal it.

"Sit down child, and I'll tell you everything."

Aubrey did as Esther said, and Esther sat in her rocking chair, taking her mind back into the past.

"I was born on a plantation before the civil war. My mama worked inside the big house where the owner lived. I was allowed to help alongside my mama, and I remember when I was five years old the owner's had a baby. A little girl named Clara."

Aubrey's eyes were growing larger.

"Clara and I grew up together, and we've known each other all of our lives. We went everywhere together and looked out for one another like best friends. Then the civil war started when we were young and grown. Henry Worthington fought in the confederacy, and was killed. He was really a wonderful man. One you could count on, who kept his promises, and never treated me like a slave. The Yankees came through and destroyed everything. They set the entire plantation on fire. I remember everyone screaming and running everywhere like ants when their hill has been disturbed. The fire spread rapidly.

Clara's mother made her leave the house, so she escaped undetected, but then the Yankees barred the doors of the house before Mrs. Worthington and my mother could get out. The Yankees didn't even care if anyone was still inside. All of this happened at night, so we couldn't really see how to help them get out. It was too late. The house became engulfed in flames, and the Yankees were still coming. Clara and I had to run through the trees in the darkness. If we hadn't, there's no telling what the Yankees would have done if they found us."

Tears streamed down both women's faces as Esther continued her nightmarish memory.

"We traveled awhile and eventually came to Moline. After losing all that we knew and loved that night, we didn't know what we were going to do, or where we were going to go. We hadn't planned on settling down in Moline, but we somehow fit in here. I was twenty-five and your mother was twenty. Not long after that we both met our husbands, and now here we are."

There was silence for a moment and then Aubrey asked, "How did you end up with his bible Esther?"

"Whenever we found out about Henry's death many weeks before the attack, my mama took his bible secretly and gave it to me."

"Why would she do that Esther?"

Esther closed her eyes.

"She took his bible and gave it to me so I would have something to remember him by. He was my pappy Aubrey."

She couldn't believe it! Esther was her aunt, her mother's sister. That explains why Esther was half white, and why she was educated which was absolutely against the law before the war. Henry must have educated her along with Clara, but now there was one more question that Aubrey needed answered.

"Does mama know about this?"

"No. All she knows is that I was a slave her papa owned."

"Esther, you've got to tell her!" Aubrey exclaimed.

"Why? Things are just fine the way they are."

"How can you keep this a secret?" Aubrey asked in disbelief.

"Neither of us like to talk about that night, and if she knew that we had the same pappy then it would crush her child. It would break her heart to know that her papa had an affair with a slave, and it might cause animosity between us if she knows I've had his bible all these years and said nothing."

"But Esther . . ."

"Aubrey child, if I tell your mama about this it would not attach two sisters, it would tear apart a good friendship. It's too late to say anything now."

Aubrey sat there shaking her head, stunned by everything she had just learned. Esther seemed intent on keeping Henry's bible and other daughter, a secret. Never before did Aubrey have a hard time keeping a secret, but since now it involved her own family members, Aubrey was torn. She could see Esther's point of view, but she didn't believe that her mother would react in the way Esther was convinced she would.

After a long silence Aubrey asked, "Esther, how did you find out that Henry was your pappy?"

"For a reason I could never explain, I always felt different from all of the other slaves. I felt sort of special. Of course I felt different from white folks because I was a slave, but I didn't really fit in with the slaves either. I found out Henry was my pappy the day mama gave me his bible, but I guess I had always suspected it somehow because he treated me the same as Clara. He just acted differently toward me than with any of the other slaves. Though when she told me I was still shocked. All the time I thought my mama's husband, a fellow slave, was my pappy, when really I was raised right there in front of him the entire time. But when I found out it was too late. He was dead and I had to keep his bible a secret."

"I can't believe he allowed you to learn."

"Me either. I didn't understand it at the time, but I guess whether I was a slave or not, as long as I was his child I would be educated."

"I'm so sorry Esther. I can't imagine going through what you have."

"It's in the past."

They gave each other an embrace, and then Aubrey headed back to the hotel. Aubrey replayed every sentence Esther said, still in shock that her ancestor lived such a life of secrecy and even deceit. Tears kept forming in her eyes, but Aubrey could not allow her mother to see that she had been crying, or Clara's curiosity would make Aubrey have to reveal the truth. Before walking back into the hotel room, Aubrey wiped her face, inhaled a deep breath, and walked inside as casually as possible.

Clara still sat where she had been sitting before Aubrey left, and when Aubrey joined her she curiously asked, "Why did you want to know about Henry Worthington?"

Aubrey was afraid this was going to happen, but she tried to answer her mother's question as carefully yet truthfully as she could.

"Um, you had never told me about my grandpa and I was just curious."

Just when Aubrey thought that she was safe from Clara's prying, Clara asked another question.

"But I've never mentioned his name before. How did you know his name?"

Aubrey didn't know what to answer. She couldn't lie, but she couldn't reveal Esther's secret either.

"What am I going to do!" she screamed within herself, trying with all of her might not to show any fear. "You know," Aubrey began to reply, hoping that the sound of her voice would ease her mother's curious mind, "I saw his name awhile back and just wondered if you knew him."

Clara could see that Aubrey was hiding something.

"Papa had never been to this town before to my knowledge. Where did you see his name?"

Aubrey was running out of explanations to pacify her mother's questions. If she explained everything to Clara, then Esther might never forgive her.

"The truth shall set you free," is what Aubrey heard the still small voice say, but she doubted that fact some in this particular situation.

"I saw his name in a bible," Aubrey finally answered, realizing that her mother was going to pry until she found out what was going on.

Now Aubrey had to leave this situation in God's hands, because she was powerless to stop the progression. Before Clara said anything else, Aubrey automatically knew what her mother would ask next.

"Whose bible?"

Aubrey took in a deep breath, pursed her lips, and then let out a very heavy sigh.

"Esther's," was all she replied.

Clara's heart sank into her stomach, as the same questions that had just eluded Aubrey now plagued her. Aubrey watched her mother's reaction and how grave she became, and just as if Aubrey had read Clara's mind, she knew what was about to happen. Clara stood to her feet, trying not to jump to any conclusions but wanting answers.

Esther had her papa's bible? Why? Anger was beginning to swell up inside of her. Was Esther a thief? Had she stolen Henry's bible long ago? Clara had believed all these years that his bible was burned along with everything else in the house the night of the Yankees raid. Aubrey knew exactly what her mother was about to do, and she had to reach Esther and warn her before Clara got to the store. Aubrey dashed in front of her mother, running as fast as she could to Esther's store. She couldn't let Esther think that she told her secret on purpose, and Aubrey hoped and prayed that Esther believed her.

People in town watched as Aubrey ran across and down the street, but she didn't care what they thought about her as she felt their wondering eyes upon her. Trying not to stumble or trip, Aubrey made it safely into the store. There were customers in the store as usual, but Aubrey went straight to Esther. Trying to keep her voice low so others would not overhear, Aubrey urgently warned Esther.

"Esther, mama is coming here right now! She knows about the bible, but not about you. I didn't mean to tell her Esther and I'm so sorry, but she kept asking questions, and . . ."

Aubrey's sentence was cut short when Clara came through the door. Aubrey had never seen her mother look so perturbed in all of her life. Esther grew serious as well.

"It's alright child. Tend to the customers for me."

She left Aubrey standing there very out of breath, and went into her room whereby Clara immediately followed her and shut the door. Aubrey began to pray that God would intervene in the situation, and not allow her mother and Esther's relationship to be severed. As she tried not to show worry on her countenance while helping customers, Aubrey listened intently for shouting or any sort of troublesome behavior, and much to her relief she heard none, however she desperately longed to know what was going on in that room.

Chapter 18

"Family Ties"

"YOU HAVE PAPA'S bible?" Clara asked boldly.

"Yes."

"Since when?" Clara snapped.

"Since the day we found out he died."

"You stole my papa's bible? Why would you do such a thing?"

Esther began shaking her head from side to side.

"I didn't steal it Clara."

"Well it was taken and you have it so you must have stolen it!" Clara said a little louder.

"Many innocent people have been persecuted because others jumped to conclusions," she stated sternly.

"Give me papa's bible," Clara demanded.

"I have as much right to it as you do."

"Excuse me? I'm his daughter, and if you didn't steal it then why is it among your things?"

Esther sighed.

"Clara, you need to sit down."

"I'd prefer to stand," Clara harshly replied.

After a long pause Esther said, "My mother gave me Henry's bible when she was told he had died."

"So your mother took it? Why?"

"Because she wanted me to have something to remember my pappy by Clara."

Clara's eyes grew wide with more shock than even Aubrey had shown. After all these years Esther's secret had finally been revealed.

"What?" was all Clara could say.

"Henry was my pappy Clara. We're sisters."

Tears formed in Clara's eyes, and she was completely at a loss for words.

"Clara, I wanted to tell you many times before honey but, there was too much at stake."

"Too much at stake? Like what?"

"Like your mother finding out, getting angry, and selling us to some other plantation. Like you being ashamed of me being your sister, and our friendship being ruined. Like you hating Henry for being unfaithful to your mother. All of those things were at stake, and I couldn't tell you. I promised my mama I would never say a word."

"I can't believe this!" Clara said in a whisper. "All of these years you knew and kept it from me."

"Clara, you have to understand my reasons. If anyone would have found out that mama took it, then there's no telling what they would've done. They might have even killed her."

Esther and Clara just stared at each other in silence for a moment. Everything made sense to Clara now. Why they were always together, why Esther was educated when none of the other slaves were allowed to learn, and why Henry had treated Esther as his own while they were growing up. Just when Esther thought that Clara was beginning to understand, Clara turned slowly and walked out of the door without saying anything more. Esther sat down in her rocking chair still clenching Henry's bible, and she cried harder than she had in years.

Aubrey watched her mother leave the store, as if she were in a daze, only staring straight ahead of her. She didn't say anything to Aubrey as she left, and this time Aubrey was sure Clara was angry with her. Aubrey walked to the door of Esther's bedroom, but listened instead of going in. She heard Esther crying through the small crack of the door, and Aubrey's heart broke.

Feeling so hurt for the two women who meant so much in her life, Aubrey depressingly went back to the counter, seeing to the customers who came in. After a while Esther finally came back out into the store. The signs of her crying were nearly all gone. When she came close, Aubrey had to say something.

"Esther, I honestly didn't mean to tell mama. She kept asking questions until I had to tell her."

Without looking up Esther replied, "This must have been the Lord's will. I know you didn't mean to tell Aubrey. I'm not upset with you."

Aubrey sighed in relief.

"You don't have to stay child. I can take care of things here."

"Are you sure you're alright?"

"Yes child. Go on."

Feeling horrible at the entire situation, Aubrey reluctantly left the store. She found herself in the same predicament she was just rescued from, and that was believing her mother was angry with her. However, Aubrey was in no way going to repeat the same actions that caused her so much heartache as before. Aubrey was going to talk to Clara and make things right, but not just yet because she wanted to give her mother time to think and cool off.

Not really knowing what to do, or where to go, Aubrey decided to pay a visit to Breu at the jailhouse. She strolled very slowly, pondering the events that had just occurred, and then the strangest thing happened.

"Sorry to hear about your brother Aubrey Whitton," a smooth and deep voice said slyly.

The man appeared out of the shadows that lurked between two buildings, and he nearly scared Aubrey to death. It was the peddler she saw that day as she rode with Breu out of town.

Gaining her composure back Aubrey replied, "Thank you Mr . . . ."

"Mr. Smith," he quickly answered.

Aubrey did not like this man's grin, because despite his exceptionally good teeth, Aubrey could sense some kind of evil intent. She also figured that Smith was not his actual name either, yet she kept that conclusion to herself.

Now that she stood a few feet away from the peddler, she could see that he was the same height as Breu, but of a thinner build. He had no facial hair, and was dressed in a businessman's suit, though Aubrey could tell that the suit was old. The peddler wore no hat and had boots on his feet, but something about him gave Aubrey the chills.

"How does this man know my name, and about my brother?" Aubrey thought. "Could he be a friend of mama or papa's?"

"Forgive me Mr. Smith but I saw you once before and you had a wagon."

"I left it in the woods where I am making my abode for now."

"I thought you had left for another town."

"I did but, there is good business here in Moline and I believe that soon I'll be hitting the jackpot."

He grinned slyly again, and Aubrey felt something urging her to go to Breu quickly. She said nothing more to the peddler, but left him standing there staring at her. His evil smirk never left his countenance and as Aubrey walked away, she wondered why he was hiding there, and why it seemed as if he had been waiting for her.

When Aubrey walked through the jailhouse door, Breu merrily welcomed his fiancé inside with a hug and kiss. Their conversation, along with Aubrey deciding that she was just being silly, made her temporarily forget about her run-in with the peddler. Kevin was spending time with his family leaving Breu all alone to handle things in town, but this didn't bother him. Breu was happy that Aubrey stopped by, though like a true lover he could see that something bothered her.

"Okay, tell me what's on your mind. I can see that something is bothering you so don't deny it."

Aubrey knew that there was no use in trying to hide what she was feeling, besides, she had gotten tired of doing that recently.

Taking in a deep breath Aubrey replied, "I'm afraid I've ruined the lives of the two women who I hold closest to me."

Breu thought for a moment and then jokingly stated, "Who? Ingrid and Rose?"

This of course made the both of them laugh which lightened the mood, but Aubrey grew serious again.

"Tell me what happened," Breu softly spoke.

"Are you sure you have enough time?"

Breu then leaned back in his sheriff's chair making it creak loudly, stretched out his legs on the floor, and raised his arms clasping his hands behind his head, all in a gesture which said to Aubrey, "I've got all the time in the world."

Aubrey told Breu everything, sparing no details. She took her time, describing the way her mother left Esther's store in silence, to the way she felt at this very moment, which was absolutely wretched. Breu's eyes widened as he listened, learning that his past wasn't the only one that consisted of murder and the destruction of people's lives as they once knew them.

Breu knew how Esther felt when it came to being one half of two ethnicities, and as Aubrey described the horrible night when her grandmother died, Breu found that he had much more in common not only with Esther, but also with Clara. Heartache was no stranger to Breu, or Esther and Clara, but it was agreeably obvious that God had pulled these two women out of their nightmare, just as He had Breu.

"I can only imagine how hard it must have been for Esther to keep that secret all these years."

"And I feel like I'm the cause of it being revealed," Aubrey explained.

"Don't worry Aubrey, Esther already said that she doesn't blame you. I'm sure your mother doesn't blame you either. Just talk to her. I'm sure she is just stunned by all of this."

"You're right, but I still can't help feeling guilty."

Breu chuckled at Aubrey and said, "My love, you are too hard on yourself."

It felt nice and encouraging to Aubrey as she talked with Breu. The way two people should feel when conversing with their mate, and the more time Aubrey spent with Breu, the more she was convinced that he was the one for her. Aubrey couldn't stay all day like she wanted to however, because Breu did have to get back to work. She figured that her mother had plenty of time alone, so when Aubrey left the sheriff's office she headed to the hotel once more to see Clara, though nervousness grew stronger with each step she took.

On the way Aubrey prayed for courage and strength to face her mother, which was something she had not done during the time before. Upon walking inside, Aubrey saw Clara with tears running down her cheeks. Clara sat on her chair and stared out through the window.

"Mama, I'm so sorry."

Aubrey really didn't know what else to say, so she listened to the silence, patiently waiting on her mother to say something.

"How long have you known?" Clara asked, still staring through the window.

"I've known that Esther had Henry Worthington's bible since we've been living in town, but I did not know who he was until a little while ago."

Aubrey answered her mother in complete and absolute honesty, hoping that Clara held nothing against her.

"Mama, are you angry with me?"

"No."

"Are you angry at Esther?"

Clara let out a heavy sigh and allowed tears to freely flow down her cheeks.

"I am not upset that she is my sister. For some unknown reason until now, I've always felt a special connection to her. I'm upset because after all these years I am just finding out about this. Most of all I'm angry with papa," Clara said shaking her head. "Why he would do such a thing! Now I'll always wonder if mother knew."

Aubrey felt tears running down her own cheeks. This was the first time Clara had ever said anything about her past to Aubrey. Aubrey even wondered if Charles knew of what her mother went through before she met him. Aubrey wanted to stay and comfort her mother, but Clara's silence was clearly telling Aubrey that she needed some time alone. Without saying anything more Aubrey quietly left the hotel room, being unsure of what to do with herself now. She was caught yet again in the middle of more family secrets, and Aubrey wanted to get away.

Not telling anyone of her plans, Aubrey started walking. It was a beautiful day for it, and Aubrey decided to solve the confusion of what to do with herself, by paying a visit to Logan. Breu was working, Clara and Esther were grieving from secrets of the past, and Charles was busy at the new house, so Aubrey confidently figured that no one would miss her.

Chapter 19

"Threat"

AUBREY VISITED WITH Mr. Benton, reminding herself that neither her mother, nor aunt blamed her for what went on in the past, or recently. It was like any other day in Moline, except for the rift that now existed between Clara and Esther, of which no one in town knew about.

Tonya Woods loved her new job, but was at home on this day because she only worked on days that Aubrey did. Ethan Bennett was happy for his love, and still left her notes in the tree after he would receive one from her. He had been busy doing chores all morning and now was finally finished. Out of curiosity, Ethan decided to go to the tree to see if there were any surprises for him. Casually he went, acting like he was inspecting the fruit, using the newly budded leaves as a cover. To his surprise a letter quietly rested in the hollow of the tree.

He wouldn't dare open the note and read it outside where his mother could possibly see, so Ethan placed the paper inside his shirt, and began walking back to the cabin, though in his heart he really wanted to run. Once inside Ethan hurried to his room and opened the note.

"Meet me in the woods in our spot at one o' clock."

This was all the entire note said, and Ethan immediately became suspicious because the handwriting wasn't Tonya's. It looked to be the same as the strange creepy note's penmanship was a while back. Something told Ethan not to go into those woods, because someone else instead of Tonya could be waiting for him there. The clock read twelve-thirty, and Ethan decided that he would go meet whoever wrote the note.

If Tonya was the one waiting on him in the woods, then wonderful, but if not, Ethan was going to confront whoever was there. Ethan knew this wasn't wise, but he could not risk causing a scene by bringing the law and having his secret revealed. Ethan knew how to use a gun, and he would be sure to bring it.

Tonya was inside the Woods home just across the fence, completely unaware of what was going on. She wasn't the one who wrote the note, and she had no idea that her life was in mortal danger. Ethan waited until no one was paying any attention, and then he ran into the woods. It was fifteen minutes until one o' clock, but Ethan couldn't wait any longer. Ethan made it safely into the woods, and hurriedly found the specific place where he and Tonya always met. Out of breath Ethan looked and called out her name, but Tonya was no where to be found.

"You made it here early," Ethan heard a man's voice say right behind him.

Ethan felt adrenaline beginning to rush through his body as his fear became reality. He turned around to see this man standing there holding a pocket watch and pointing a pistol right at him.

"Who are you and what do you want?" Ethan demanded.

"Who I am isn't important and I want gold."

Ethan had no idea what this man was talking about, and he had confusion on his countenance.

"I heard that the Whittons have a secret goldmine. Is that true?"

"I wouldn't know," Ethan sternly replied.

The man put a smirk on his face.

"Well I believe it is true, and you are going to take me to Aubrey Whitton, or Tonya dies."

What was Ethan going to do! If he helped this man then Aubrey's life was in danger, however if Ethan didn't, then he and Tonya's lives would be. How did this strange man know about Ethan and Tonya? How did he know of where they met?

"You're the one who wrote that note aren't you?"

The man only smiled.

"So you have been watching us. Tell me something, why do you want me to help you?"

"I've been observing Moline and its lowly people for quite some time now, and what I have discovered is that Aubrey trusts you. You are my ticket to her, and she is my ticket to the gold."

"And what if you're wrong about the gold?" Ethan asked.

"I'm never wrong. Now if you will cooperate then you and your little girlfriend won't be hurt. Drop your gun belt."

Though he didn't want to, Ethan had to do what this man said. He slowly loosened his gun belt and let it fall to the ground.

"Now where would Aubrey be right now?"

"I have no idea," Ethan said loudly.

The man smirked again and said, "Well then we'll just have to look for her. Move!" he commanded, and Ethan's mind was racing trying to figure out what to do.

Ethan began walking, going where ever the man told him to. First he had to get this man away from Tonya so she would be safe, then he would figure out a way to escape and warn Aubrey, but how he would do this Ethan still did not know.

There was one thing that Ethan was certain of, he did not know who this man was, because he had never seen before, however, if Aubrey had been there she would have known him definitely as Mr. Smith.

Chapter 20

"Search"

THE PEDDLER DIRECTED Ethan to where he kept his wagon, and he made Ethan unhitch the two horses that pulled the wagon. Ethan knew that it would not take long for his family to begin wondering where he was, so he took his time when the peddler gave him a command. The pistol's aim was kept on Ethan at all times, and soon they were on the horses traveling into town.

Now that they were a good distance from Tonya, Ethan was going to try to get away from the peddler the first chance he could. The peddler had observed enough in Moline to know that Aubrey stayed with Esther in her store, so he told Ethan they were going there first.

When they arrived at the store, the peddler hid his pistol in his jacket still pointing it at Ethan, and he would not allow Ethan to go in by himself. Esther could tell that something was wrong when Ethan and the peddler asked about Aubrey. She could see on Ethan's countenance that he was uncomfortable and even worried.

"I haven't seen her child," she replied giving Ethan a curious look. This was all she answered.

"Thanks Esther," Ethan said, but what she was unaware of was that he was really thanking her for not giving up Aubrey's whereabouts, whether she honestly knew where she was or not.

The peddler gave Esther a smirk before he followed Ethan back out to the horses, which gave Esther a very uneasy feeling. She noticed that Ethan wasn't his normal self, and she kept her eyes on them until they were out of sight. Then she ran across the street to go alarm Breu.

"Breu!" Esther said in between heavy breaths. "I think Ethan, and maybe Aubrey are in trouble."

Breu stood to his feet. She described everything that had just happened, and as soon as she finished, the first thing that came to Breu's mind was the note Ethan brought him a while ago.

Breu was certain these two situations were linked, so he thanked Esther for the information, and then ran to the hotel to talk to Clara.

"Do you know where she went?" he asked her, trying not to sound too excited once in the hotel room.

"She didn't say," Clara told him. "She just left. Is everything alright?"

"Yes ma'am, but if she does come back, please tell her to wait here for me."

"Of course Breu," Clara agreed.

If she wasn't with Clara or Esther, then Brue had only a handful of places where she could be. Either she was out at the Whitton place with Charles, in the meadow, at Logan's cabin, or at the gazebo. Breu jumped onto his horse and decided to go see Charles first.

He galloped his horse, making the horse run as fast as he could while he held on tightly to the reins. Breu was extremely anxious to get to Charles, because he hoped with all of his might that Aubrey was there. Finally he arrived and he came to a stop. Without even getting off of his horse he asked Charles if he'd seen Aubrey.

"No I haven't."

"Could she be in the meadow?"

"No. I would have seen her pass by."

Breu's heart sank, and he felt the blood drain from his face. He tried to remain calm, because after all, Aubrey could possibly be safe and sound. "Thanks Charles," Breu said, but before Charles could say anything else, Breu had already begun galloping away. Charles thought that was peculiar, but he kept working. However, the longer he stayed there working, the more uneasy he began to feel.

Aubrey had another wonderful visit with Logan. When she left Mr. Benton's cabin, she decided to go sit a while at the gazebo to think and talk with God. The last thing in her mind was that her life was in jeopardy. Charles set his tools on the floor of the future house, then left to go see if Clara knew what was going on with Aubrey and Breu. Charles had been gone only a few moments when Ethan and the peddler rode up to where Charles had just been working.

"Mr. Whitton!" Ethan shouted, hoping he wasn't there.

Without waiting or asking for permission from the peddler, he jumped down from his horse, acting as though he was really looking for Charles as he kept shouting his name, when actually Ethan sought some way to escape.

Before long Ethan spotted Charles' hammer that was lying on the floor. Swiftly he grabbed it and threw the hammer at the peddler, using all of the force he possessed. He hit the peddler dead on, knocking him off of his horse. Ethan sprinted toward the peddler so he could take the gun away from him, but as he speedily approached, the peddler pulled his gun out and shot Ethan! His speed wasn't fast enough in this situation, and now he lay in excruciating pain on the ground.

The peddler rubbed his chest due to the pain the hammer's pound had caused, and then he jumped onto his horse and galloped away, leaving Ethan there bleeding on the ground. The peddler had heard of this Mr. Logan Benton through persistent and sly observations of Aubrey and Breu. Though he hadn't been there, he heard enough to figure out where Mr. Benton's place existed. As cunning as the peddler was, it did not take him long to find it, but he saw the sheriff speaking with the old man.

There was yet another place the peddler could look, and that was at the gazebo of which he had heard alot about also. Little did Aubrey and Breu know in days passed, that while they were thinking the peddler was peddling in some other town, he really wasn't. He had been sneakily eavesdropping on their conversations. So yet again, the peddler found the gazebo, and he saw a young lady sitting inside.

Rose Bennett stood outside of her cabin with her arms crossed, looking in every direction for her son. She kept calling his name as loudly as she could, but there was no sign of him. His younger siblings had not seen him either. Rose was becoming upset, and she decided that when Ethan did make his appearance, he would certainly be in trouble. How ironic it was that Ethan already was in dire need of help, and his mother had no idea!

Aubrey sat there in the gazebo with her eyes closed enjoying the peaceful songs of the birds, when she heard the hammer of a gun being pulled back right behind her. Immediately her eyes sprung open, and when she turned around she saw the peddler smirking as he pointed his pistol at her.

"Now don't make any sounds Aubrey. Come get on this horse, or my face will be the last one you'll ever see again."

Aubrey wanted to start crying. Surely this wasn't really happening all over again! But it was, because she couldn't just imagine something like this.

"Hurry now Aubrey, I haven't got all day."

She did as the peddler said, because there was no way she could defend herself against a bullet. If only she had known that Breu was close enough to hear her scream, then she could have somehow stalled, having Breu discover the two, but she had absolutely no idea about Breu being near, or Ethan being shot.

Aubrey climbed onto the horse having to sit in front of the peddler, and he took off, galloping back to the Whitton property. She began praying in her heart, because Aubrey was scared out of her mind. They galloped until they came to the Whitton's place, then Aubrey screamed when she saw Ethan lying on the ground. He looked dead!

The peddler galloped passed the beginnings of a house, going in the direction of the meadow. Tears began pouring out of her eyes because of Ethan lying helplessly on the ground and there being no way for her to help him. After riding a while longer, the peddler brought the horse to a halt in the meadow. He jumped down, and Aubrey was forcefully pulled down as well.

No one was around save the peddler, his horse, and Aubrey. She could see Marty's grave from where they now stood, and they were surrounded by trees. All was peaceful and quiet, until the peddler spoke.

"Alright Aubrey. I've heard lots of talk about there being a goldmine here with more than enough riches to spoil a man. If you'll show me where it is then I'll gladly take it and be on my way."

"How unwise to commit such unlawful acts when you have only heard that there is gold here," Aubrey bravely stated.

"Oh come now Aubrey," he said with that evil smirk she had become familiar with, "you know as well as I that gold is here."

He made a motion with his head to Marty's grave which cut like a knife through Aubrey's heart.

"The men who rode with your brother are in prison now. The same prison in fact where I just came from. They told me their suspicions of gold being here."

"Just how do you know so much about me?" Aubrey asked with anger in her eyes.

"I've stayed in town long enough to learn all I need to know about you. Now show me where the gold is, and I'll let you go."

"First tell me about Ethan," Aubrey demanded.

"He was supposed to lead me to you but he had other plans. You see where that got him."

Terror gripped Aubrey, and she decided right then and there that gold, no matter what amount, wasn't worth anyone's life. Ethan was lying out there dying, if he wasn't already dead, and her life was now on the line.

"Alright. I'll take you to the gold if you will leave afterward and never return."

"As you wish," the peddler smirked taking a bow.

"It's still a little way from here so we've got to get on the horse," Aubrey informed as she hurriedly got back on the horse's back.

The peddler speedily jumped back on as well being happy that Aubrey wasn't going to give him any trouble, but this time Aubrey took the reins and they began galloping. She didn't care anymore. She had to get back to Ethan before it was too late.

Aubrey did have one thing up her sleeve however. When Charles first started mining in the hills, he found gold right inside the entrance, which is where he began to dig, but it was fool's gold. Charles discovered this later, and almost gave up on gold mining, but the further into the hills he mined, the more gold he found, and it was real. She was going to show him the fools gold, because it was plenteous, and the peddler wouldn't know the difference. He would be able to get more than he could possibly carry, so as they got to the hills and jumped off of the horse, Aubrey led him inside. Charles kept a lantern against the wall just as you walk in, so the peddler took a match from his jacket and lit it.

The brighter the flame in the lantern, the more sparkles and shimmers vibrantly pulsated from the wall. Aubrey watched the peddler's expression, and he believed that he had just hit the jackpot.

"Here it is," Aubrey said, but she started to walk away so she could go to Ethan.

"Where do you think you are going?" the peddler asked.

"I've got to help him. He could die!" Aubrey exclaimed.

"He should have thought about that sooner. I'm not done with you yet so just sit down right over there," he said pointing at a large round rock. Aubrey wanted to take off running, but she knew that she would never make it. Tears poured out of her eyes again because she could not get to Ethan. Her heart pounded, her blood raced through her veins, and Aubrey was helpless, but not entirely. As the peddler began prying away at the rock and clay, Aubrey closed her eyes and began to pray.

Breu had to see for himself that Aubrey wasn't in the meadow after he couldn't find her at the gazebo, so as he made his way up to the Whitton house still expecting to see Charles, Ethan is who he saw lying on the ground. Breu jumped down from his horse and ran to Ethan.

"He's got her," Ethan cried. "The peddler. He's got Aubrey. They're looking for the gold."

Ethan was suffering with incredible pain.

"I've got to get you to the doctor."

"No no. I'm only shot in the shoulder. Just give me something to stop the bleeding and I'll wait here. You've got to help Aubrey."

Breu quickly rummaged through his saddle bag and pulled out several rags. He packed them together in a wad, placed it on Ethan's wound, and set him on the newly built porch of the Whitton house. Back on his horse he got and galloped to the hills. He pushed his horse to the limit as far as speed is concerned, and soon he arrived at the goldmine. Breu tried to be quiet as he got off of his animal, set him free, and listened at the edge of the entrance on the outside. Breu thought he could hear something, but wasn't sure.

Just as he was about to enter the mine, he heard someone approaching the entrance. Pressing his back tightly against the side of the hill, the peddler walked out with his hands full of gold, but he never even detected Breu.

Having his gun drawn Breu said, "Turn around and don't move."

The peddler stopped dead in his tracks, doing just as Breu said and slowly turned around with a smirk on his face. Without taking his eyes off of the peddler Breu shouted for Aubrey. She heard his voice, and she felt such a flooding of relief and excitement as she rushed outside to him.

"Breu!" she shouted as she ran to him.

"Aubrey, take the peddler's horse and go get Kevin. Ethan needs help."

Without saying another word Aubrey did as she was told.

"Wait," Breu said, "step aside ten feet," he commanded the peddler, because he couldn't risk the peddler grabbing Aubrey and using her against him. With a devious wicked look the peddler moved aside. Aubrey got on his horse and galloped away.

She came to Ethan and saw him suffering on the porch. He looked relieved to see that she was alright. She got down and ran to him.

"Do you think you can get on the horse?" she asked very out of breath.

"Yes but I may need some help."

She wrapped her arm around his waist and his unwounded arm around her neck. They struggled, but once Ethan was on his feet things got easier. Aubrey helped him onto the horse despite his large size, then she climbed up and sat behind him. She could not see over his large broad shoulders, so struggling she moved from side to side looking around his body so she could see where they were going. They galloped toward town, and Aubrey was going to drop him off at the doctor's office before she alerted Kevin of what was happening.

Breu whistled for his horse, and eventually retrieved the reins without losing sight of the peddler. He climbed on the horse's back, and was going to make the peddler walk. As he slowly directed the horse close to the peddler, still pointing his gun, the peddler threw the gold pieces that he held in his hand into Breu's face, and pushed Breu off of the horse. Breu lost his gun, and a wrestling match started between the two.

Neither Breu nor the peddler could see very well because of all of the dirt and punches. Everytime Breu had his gun within reach, the peddler attacked him, making the gun move even further away. Blood was getting mixed up with the dirt, and both men were covered in grime.

After what seemed like an eternity of fighting the men were wearing down, and Breu thought he saw someone riding up, however he didn't have time to look because the peddler was still swinging. Out of the blue, Breu heard a gunshot, and then the world seemed to freeze. When Breu looked he saw the peddler laying dead on the ground, and Charles standing beside his horse with smoke escaping out of his gun.

Charles had searched in town but no one knew where Aubrey was, so he decided to investigate for himself. As he approached the hills he had seen Breu and another man fighting, so he shot the peddler. Breu was bleeding in his face, and he was never more glad to see Charles.

"You alright?" Charles asked.

"I am now."

"Where's Aubrey?"

"She went to go get Kevin."

"So she's alright?" Charles asked in concern.

"Yes she's alright. Ethan isn't though. He's been shot in the shoulder. I left him on your porch."

"I didn't see him when I came through."

"Aubrey must have taken him back to town then," Breu stated as he dusted himself off.

He was shook up and a little unsteady on his feet.

"Well, let's load him up and get him back to town," Charles said.

Both men grabbed an end of the peddler and draped him over Breu's horse like a lifeless blanket. Soon they were on their way, but since the danger was over Charles and Breu took their time. They discussed everything that happened, and as they rode Deputy Kevin came galloping to them very excitedly.

"What happened?"

"Charles came to my rescue, so he beat you!" Breu joked. "It's a good thing too because I don't know how much longer I could have fought him until you got here."

"So everything is alright," Kevin asked again, this time looking down at the dead body Breu's horse carried.

"Yes, I'll explain on the way."

Aubrey sat beside Ethan and watched as Dr. Starks removed the bullet. There was alot of blood, but the bullet was carefully removed and the wound cleaned. As the men came riding back into town, so did Rose Bennett.

She looked at the dead body on Breu's horse and snidely said, "So you've killed someone else huh?"

"No I did," Charles snapped back. "Now why don't you go see your son and mind your own business."

They all figured that someone from town rode out to the Bennett's and informed Rose of her son's condition. She rolled her eyes at Charles' remark and made her way to the doctor's office.

A few moments later as Ethan rested and Aubrey held his hand, the door to the office busted open and Rose Bennett came inside, acting more dramatic than Aubrey had ever seen her act before.

"Oh Ethan my poor baby!" she whaled.

She began crying and turning the situation into an unnecessary drama. "What are you doing here? I thought I told you to stay away from my son!" she screamed at Aubrey.

Aubrey didn't know what to say, but even if she did she wouldn't have been able to say it because of Rose's boisterous tantrum.

"How did he get shot?" she demanded to know from someone.

By now Kevin, Charles, and Breu had entered the doctor's office and could see her actions.

Very calmly and quietly Aubrey replied, "Rose, Ethan was shot because he was protecting me."

Instead of Rose being proud of the bravery of her son, she took her anger about his injury out on Aubrey.

"I knew that if you didn't stay away from him then something like this would happen!" she shouted.

Charles, Breu, and Kevin were growing angry at Rose's tirade and stopped themselves several times from walking over there and getting in her face. Ethan was terribly embarrassed and upset with the way his mother was acting.

"Mama stop it now!" he shouted back.

Aubrey left the doctor's office in shock, and Doctor Starks warned Rose that if she didn't calm down then he would ask Kevin to escort her out. Whether Ethan was her son or not, he was Doctor Starks' patient and she was upsetting him. Finally after Aubrey, Breu, and Charles left, Rose began to calm down and desist with the drama. Aubrey had her arms crossed and couldn't believe the way Rose just treated her.

"I'm going to go let Clara know that everything is alright," Charles informed as he walked away.

Tears stung Aubrey's eyes as Breu looked into her face.

"Aubrey, don't listen to that woman. She is nothing but a brawler and what she said isn't true."

"Breu, Ethan was almost killed because of me. He was protecting me and almost lost his life. Why are people after me and this gold? Why are the ones I care about getting hurt? I thought that with Marty's death came the end of all this greed and trouble, but now someone else has gotten hurt. What am I going to do? If that peddler had killed Ethan I . . . I . . ."

"But he didn't. God was protecting him and you. You can't dwell on what could have been."

Breu took her into his arms and held her tightly.

"The gold is supposed to be a secret Breu. If that peddler knew about it then who else may know?"

He understood what she was saying, but he had no answers to any of her questions.

"There is only one thing I can do," Aubrey finished. "One of us is going to have to go. Either me or the gold."